real teens

Diary of a Junior Year

volume 5

SCHOLASTIC INC.
New York Toronto London Auckland Sydney
Mexico City New Delhi Hong Kong

ISBN 0-439-08412-1

Distributed under license from
The Petersen Publishing Company, L.L.C.
Copyright © 2000 The Petersen Publishing
Company, L.L.C. All rights reserved.
Published by Scholastic Inc.

Produced by 17th Street Productions, Inc.
33 West 17th Street
New York, NY 10011

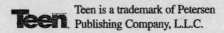

Teen is a trademark of Petersen
Publishing Company, L.L.C.

12 11 10 9 8 7 6 5 4 3 2 1   0 1 2 3 4/0 5/0

Printed in the U.S.A.   01
First Scholastic Printing, March 2000

Special thanks to Laura Dower

Diary of a Junior Year

volume 5

The diaries you are about to read are real. Names, places, and other details have been changed to protect the teens involved. But what they have to say all really happened.

Marybeth Miller:

I'm a wiseass. I can make just about anyone smile, even if they're feeling down in the dumps, and that's really important 2 me. Some days I consider myself fatter than others, but what are you gonna do, right? I run track and play basketball and keep on—so it's no big deal. Mostly I love just hanging out with my friends. Mom, Dad, and my brother and sister r cool 2, I guess. I mean, we don't <u>always</u> get along, but I pull thru. I don't think I would want anything else.

<u>LIKES</u>: My yellow Polo shirt

<u>DISLIKES</u>: People who can't take a joke

Billy Shim:

I'm an outgoing, crazy guy, but I have mixed feelings about it. I'm smart and get good grades, but I know that's not good enough so I need something that stands out like sports, sports, sports! The scene with my parents is totally up/down. We have great moments, but we have arguments too—like good grades = heaven and bad grades = hell. But my older brother Lee, who's playing football at college right now, he's always there for me. Lee is the nicest guy you could ever meet. I think things would be easier if I were more like him.

   LIKES: Sports, sports, sports (esp. lacrosse in spring)

   DISLIKES: Stupid, clingy chicks

Teresa Falcone:

   There is much more going on in my mind than the eye can see. . . . I love writing, reading, dancing, singing, acting, playing field hockey, listening to all kinds of music, and most of all being with my friends and family. I know I'm smart and get really good grades, but I have this problem, which is everyone sees me as this airhead. I hate that! Sometimes I can be sooooo insecure! My parents are divorced, so I live with my mom and my older brother Vincent, even though we don't get along ever. My dad lives a town away, so I see him a lot.

<u>LIKES</u>: Romance books and anything else romantic!

<u>DISLIKES</u>: Not being taken seriously!

<u>Jake Barosso:</u>

Ladies think I'm cute, but only sometimes. I'm shy, but I love to dance and I'm always on the go. I love raving, riding a Jet Ski, playing pool, and fixing up my new car. My dad is really really sick, so things are terrible at home right now, but I try to help out as much as I can. We're always arguing about the stupidest things. I wish it didn't have to be like this. I like to make Mom + sis laugh whenever I can. I'm funny too.

<u>LIKES:</u> My car!!!

<u>DISLIKES:</u> Being sick + people who are assholes (a tie)

<u>Katie Carson:</u>

I am involved in Community Club and student council, on the tennis team, and a peer ministry leader of my church, among other things. To fit it all into one word, I am well-rounded. My schedule is nuts, but I handle stress with my sense of humor. I have important long-term goals for myself. Sometimes my friends tell me I am naive about things, but I really do believe I have the ability to get along with <u>everyone</u>. The most important thing to me is family— we're very close and share a special bond. I can tell my mom everything.

   <u>LIKES:</u> Musical theater, travel, good grades, Brad

   <u>DISLIKES:</u> People who don't have any goals

<u>Edward</u> <u>Baxter:</u>

This is me. I'm all the characteristics associated with this picture. I love listening to music, watching TV, and playing Nintendo. I'm a yearbook editor, sometimes I run track and I'm in Community Club, even though I'm starting to hate it, and I mean REALLY HATE IT. I'm also a bad speller, but for the most part I do well in school. As far as parents go, mine

5

are like big kids. My dad is a real comedian and my mom is stupid funny, like me. My older brother Jerry is away at college.

<u>LIKES:</u> Coconut my dog

<u>DISLIKES:</u> People who never call you back, especially when you beep them

Emma West:

I think I'm totally trustworthy, kind, and respectful, but if someone starts talking about me behind my back I feel a lot different and I get upset. At school I'm ice-hockey manager and I'm in community Club and student council. I love hanging out but I usually don't make any plans until like the last minute, usually with marybeth. The most important thing is that my friends mean the world to me. my parents are cool too. They're always running around doing a million different things and my little brother Ronnie thinks he runs the house. my sister Lynn and I have to babysit for nim

a lot, which can be a drag but whatever.
  LIKES: Having a boyfriend
  DISLIKES: Being left out

Kevin Moran:
    I'm all this: smart, funny, hyper,
and I don't know what else kind of
guy. I kinda go from one thing to
another like wave running, clubbing,
swimming, mainly any sport—and mostly
just chilling with my friends. Still,
I get bored all the time. My
family, they're loud, and Dad has
been married 2x so we have a lotta
freakin people here to deal with
and we argue like ALL THE TIME
but that's cool I guess cuz I
really do love them all. I was
really close to my sis Lena, but she
died like 8 years ago when I was 8,
which still makes me mad.
    LIKES: Dressing and doing stuff
exactly as I want it and no one
can tell me anything else
    DISLIKES: My brother Neil no
doubt!

7

Billy

Well, today is Valentine's Day and I don't have a
valentine. I was hoping that there was a chance I
might hook up with Olivia again even though I knew
she would prob. be w/her boyfriend or something.
But I can still hope, can't I? Esp. after us clicking on
the bus last time we were together and her calling for
me every time I got up to walk somewhere at the
party. Maybe I have that effect on all women & I just
need the beer to bring it out.

There is another girl that I truly cherish and that is
Shauna Hirsh. I haven't told anyone about this one. She
also is seeing this guy, the ugliest kid I have ever seen. I
can't stand him. I wanted Shauna like crazy last year but
couldn't have her and now apparently she's single but I
don't trust that. I just have to face that the two girls I want
have boyfriends or pending boyfriends or boyfriends who
won't go away and so I just have to keep it cool. As usual I
feel really hypocritical about shit. I want things and then I
don't want things, like good grades or doing well in football and now Olivia and Shauna.

Rehearsals are coming up this week for the show. I
am supposed to practice more but I can't really help
with the set or anything b/c of my arm. It still hurts. I
am trying more therapy w/my doc but who knows
when it will be cured. I just have to deal and stop
whining about it. The whole thing is a mess.

8

Emma

Right now I am getting ready to go out w/Cliff for Valentine's Day. He took off from work or changed his shift so we could be together. Isn't that sweet? I am so happy about that. Things are good with us right now. I made reservations for us to go to this Beef and Brew place in town because he loves that place. The best part is that I didn't tell him I made any reservations until this morning, so he was wicked surprised. I thought it was a cute thing to do because he loves to eat there and so I planned it. Dinner is at like 5 o'clock so I am going to go pick him up in like an hour or so. I want to look good for him. I got him this card that says "I want to get you out of my thoughts" on the front, and then inside it says "And into my arms." My cousin picked it out and it is so perfect for me and Cliff. I signed it "Love always, Em," and that's it. I didn't want to get too mushy because we've only been together for 2 months. Whatever. On Feb. 27 it will be 3 months. Yeah! I am so glad to have someone today. Gotta go!

Teresa

Feb 14

Dear Diary,

Well, the crappy day is here! Happy *ucking Valentine's Day, pardon my French. Ever since last year, I have had a grudge against Valentine's Day. Last year I was seeing this kid Nino and I had presents for him and everything but he just never asked me to do anything on the day. So I was really pissed off and I went to this club nearby where they were having this big party, and I cheated on him. I just put all my anger there and I know it was the wrong thing to do but still. So now all I think about Valentine's Day is that it's such a cheesy, corny holiday. And yes, I probably wouldn't be saying this if I had someone, but that's besides the point.

Despite how pathetic this night had the potential to be, however, I actually had a good time. During the day I went shopping to buy an outfit for what I did tonite, which was go to this teen party at Club Clove. Me and my field-hockey buddy Stephanie went and had a good amount of fun! The place was *packed* but we managed to keep a spot on the dance floor the whole night. The good thing about it was that we knew the guys there would be single. I mean, why else would they be at a club on Valentine's Day?!

I ended up finding and seeing that guy Jesse I know from hockey, the one I hooked up with in January. Well, he has a girlfriend, I know that much, but obviously she wasn't there tonite. Obviously they're not too happy because he handed me a teddy bear that said "I Love You" when I saw him. It was so cute. I wonder what that means? I was thinking maybe V-Day isn't so bad after all.

Anyway, later on I also smiled at this other really hot guy and at one point he smiled back! Then he grabbed my hand and we started dancing together. I'm mad though because I never got his name. But me & Stephanie got flyers for the next teen night that's planned @ the club, which is in April. We are *definitely* going.

Katie

February 15
Presidents' Day (no school)
@ 9 A.M.

Valentine's Day was special but nothing like I had anticipated it to be. I have now confirmed that it is, indeed, a stupid holiday. It is so glorified and for what? I can't even express its stupidity. Sure, the roses and whatever are nice, but the truth is that for me and Brad it is no different than all our other days together. He did try to make yesterday *extra* special, though, which was nice.

My day (Feb. 14) began with an SAT tutor and that was awful. I hate the SATs. Afterward I just cleaned up my room and hung out until about four or so, when I decided to shower and get dressed. I did something today that I originally had thought of as a small gesture but it turned into something big. Like two weeks ago I had ordered a Valentine's Day heart-o-gram for Gwen. She's been upset lately because she doesn't have a boyfriend right at the moment and swim team isn't going well and school is just tough these days. She did much better on tennis team in the fall. So I figured I could "be her valentine" like as a joke. I drove over to her house to drop it off (it was a huge bunch of heart balloons) and she and her parents had *just* pulled into the driveway. I guess she had been crying because she lost the 100-meter relay or something. Well, when she saw me she couldn't believe it. She hugged me so hard and I was so glad that I had done that. Her mom even said they'd been trying to cheer her up all the way home and nothing worked. Anything for a friend!

After I left Gwen's, I met up with Brad. It was nice because he gave me a stuffed teddy bear holding a rose, a giant balloon that says "I Love *YOU*," and a box of Godiva chocolates. It's certainly the right time of the month for *those*! I got him some boxer shorts, a mug & T-shirt, and some other little stuff. I also wrote him a really sappy letter, which is not really characteristic of me, but I did it anyway. I needed to let him know how I felt. Then we hopped in the car, went out for Thai food, and decided to head down to the beach house just because it seemed like a romantic thing to do. What we ended up doing was taking four blankets out of the car, dragging them out onto the sand, and curling up to keep warm. We just held each other.

p.s. For fun Friday at school we did this data match in order to find out who is our most compatible partner. Unbelievably I got Kevin, which is so weird since we haven't really been talking much this year. Teresa seemed annoyed by the whole thing. I think she's just mad about Valentine's Day for some reason. This is who I matched up with:

```
Top Love Matches for Kathryn Carson
              From Grade 11
% Compatibility   Grade     Name
      73.246%      11    Kevin Moran  How weird!
      69.882%      11    Carlos Diaz  Class brain
      61.252%      11    Edward Baxter  ?!!!!!
      54.545%      11    Jonny Marshall
      51.545%      11    Alex White  My coanchor!
      46.346%      11    Richard Wright  Should
                                     I tell MB
                                     about this one?
```

So that was an interesting thing to see on Valentine's Day. It turns out that my best match of all in the whole school is a ninth grader! Now *that's* really weird, right?

Kevin

I was sick yesterday and felt like total shit it was soooo bad, my throat was all sore it was not fun at all. I think maybe I caught something on Fri. when I was working teaching kids to swim really it isn't work I love it too much for that. After I got home I drank like 5 liters of soda to try and flush it out of me and slept a lot too. But last nite I went to this mad party at May's place and b/c she has a pool table like a ton of people showed up there, like too many people to even explain. And b/c I was sick, I was the designated driver but if I wasn't the designated driver I still would have gone to the party maybe skated over like Jake did *LOL* ha ha. So anyways someone said holy shit there were like all these cops around and so we were freakin out. Ok so then we are like driving around a little and someone else stops the car and says that there really were cops there and they busted everything up. Ohhh man I was lookin for Jake everywhere but we couldn't find him it was weird. Later on I found out he was ok but man what a weird thing with people running all over the place. Ok and then for the actual Valentine's Day thing I did nothing. My mom never told me what I should get her so I decided to just go & buy this joke present and that is something I am definitely good at he he he. So I got her all this joke sex stuff from this store at the mall

14

like this fake bondage starter set with massage oil and fuzzy handcuffs and wrote on the card "For you and Dad, Happy Valentine's Day, Love, Kev." She was dying I haven't seen her laugh that hard maybe ever. I was glad I could make her laugh.

So I really wanted to see Rosie sooo bad on Valentine's Day nite but decided it was way better not to make her sick or anything. Since I couldn't hang w/her me, Jake, and Micky Lazlo went to May's again to shoot pool and just hang out again. It was cool fun. Mick was hanging with us b/c his gf Deb was grounded from the night before. Ok then so after a while it got pretty boring actually and we just chilled b/c we were tired as hell soooo that was that and now today I am just restin up b/c we have no school ok ta ta.

Here's part of something I downloaded for whatever reason:

24. One word—*foreplay.*
25. Buy gifts for each other.
26. Even more roses.
27. Incense/candles/oils/black lights/music make for great cuddling/sex.
28. Lightly kiss her collarbone or jawbone or stomach.
29. Smell her hair.
30. Write poetry for each other.
31. Tell her that she's the only girl you want. Don't lie.

32. Keep one of her bras somewhere you see it every day.
33. Sing to each other.
34. Unless you can feel her heart beating, you aren't close enough.
35. PDA = public display of affection.
36. Be Prince Charming to her parents.
37. Read to each other.
38. French-kiss again.
39. Walk behind her and put your hands in her front pockets.

Jake

February 15

Well, Valentine's was just like any other day for me because of course I have no woman that can care for me. I saw no flowers and hearts and kisses. And I tried not to let it bother me, but it did.

There was a party the other night at May's house and I was there. I got pretty plastered on like three beers and about ten shots of vodka. I was *really* drunk but I was having a damn good time. Then what happened is these stupid little eighth graders came and said that there were cops on the way and so everyone jetted out of there like fast. I went through the back door and jumped the fence. I actually got cut bad on my wrist because of the fence and I think

16

I'll probably get a bad scar there. Then I ended up with some seniors and we drove around for a while to see if things would cool down. When we got back to the party, people were still saying the cops were cruising around, so I left again. I went over to the Silverado because I was getting hungry. I think I saw Kevin leaving through the front and coming to look for me, but we were gone by then.

Marybeth

February 15th

I'm hanging out at home right now b/c there is no school due to Presidents' Day holiday, which is excellent. Let's see what's been going on, well on Friday was a basketball game & then I was supposed to babysit but nothing worked out 2 good. So a few of us girls just went to eat & then over to May's for a party, which was ok I guess, decent. Sat. morning I got up so early to go feed the homeless & then get a haircut, which was *HORRIBLE* but it's better now. Sat. afternoon I had to work but went to another party later on. It was @ May's place again. I think her parents are away for like 3 weeks or something. I got drunk. And then someone yelled, *"COPS,"* and we all ran like everywhere. I jumped like 3 fences it was crazy . . . and as it turns out there were no cops, which I can't believe! That just sucked. But I still say it was an A+ party anyway even tho the cops came it was all good.

Yesterday for Valentine's Day my daddy bought me flowers. He gave me this card too. He is so cute. He made Mom and me dinner too.

Be my valentine, sweetheart!
Love, Dad

Tonite I was supposed to go back to May's again just to play pool, Kevin asked me to meet him and some others over there, but Mom said no. I'm pretty sure that she knew I had been drinking so I stayed home and we just talked. I was of course freaking out b/c of everything that's been goin on w/us. She is 2 overprotective & she gets so pissed at me and doesn't trust me 4 anything! I tried to tell her again that when I go out I am being honest w/her about where I am going and what I am doing. And she was like, Look, I know you do and I want to trust u sometimes but I can't. I said to her if she won't trust me then it almost makes me feel like why not lie 2 her then? But I dunno all in all it was still a good convo I guess. We talked at least, like there was no yelling. I felt like this time she was really listening 2 me.

Baxter

February 15

Yesterday was no big deal. I was right again about Valentine's Day. I thought maybe I would get something for Megan or even Jessica or maybe send one of those electronic e-mail cards but I decided not to. I decided just to pretend as if Valentine's Day did not exist. I just keep telling myself it's no big deal. Not everyone has a valentine anyway.

I still have not found out who stole those candy bars from me last week, and I am still angry about it. Once again things are not working out for the best. For some reason everything is against me, or at least that is how it feels to me. Grades are better again though.

I promised Emma I would give her a call tonight. She wasn't sure about one of the homework assignments. I like talking to her on the phone. It should cheer me up. She will probably tell me I should just go for it and ask Megan out. She always says that to me. I don't know what stops me from just doing that. I don't know!!!!

Taking Risks Taking Risks

Teresa:
   I wish I could take more emotional risks, like with guys, but it's just so hard for me to get close both mentally and physically. I am not sure why maybe it's just that I have this great fear of rejection. Maybe I can't risk giving any parts of myself away because unconsciously inside I am afraid of something happening like what happened with my parents. I mean, they said they were in love but then they fell out of love and got divorced.

Kevin:
   I don't REALLY think of things like I Am tAkin RiSkS I juSt SAy if Something doesn't woRK out At leASt I hAd fun doin it. I don't need to do theSe mAjoR things to mAke Anyone elSe hAppy I juSt wAnnA be SAtiSfied foR mySelf And 4 me it's no big RiSk juSt bein mySelf.

Taking Risks Taking Risks

Katie:

I think that as junior year has gone on, I have been able to take more chances and risks just being myself and standing up for what I believe is right. I think sometimes I am really naive and so it's a risk for me to just put myself out there when everyone around me is drinking and dressing differently. I am more conservative, don't drink, etc.

Jake:

If a risk needs to be taken then I will take it. I want to succeed very much.

Billy:

I don't think I take enough risks b/c I am afraid of losing. And then I just lie awake at night and I think, am I doing everything I need to be doing? What if I make choices that risk where I will live or work or go to college? What if I don't risk enough?

21

Taking Risks Taking Risks

<u>Marybeth:</u>

Well, I wrote that speech for community club about taking risks & chances & putting it all out there and that is how I feel 100%. Other random risks I have taken include trying to smoke (the 1st time I ever did it I got nothing out of it my teeth were dirty and I was looking for gum). Then the 1st time I drank it was a risk too b/c I was a beginner & I had to figure out how much I could drink w/out getting caught by my mother.

<u>Baxter:</u>

I should try to express myself better sometimes. I think it is very good to let out my feelings instead of keeping them bottled up.

<u>Emma:</u>

I will not risk getting caught by my parents or anyone else for doing something I am not supposed to do. no way!!!

Billy

My mom got me a new mouse so now it's easier to type @ the computer keyboard with my arm being a mess. It's 10:45 right now and I just finished watching TV. Today was pretty boring, nothing really happened. Well, one little thing happened. When I went to school, as soon as I got there the fire alarm came on. It was just 8 and school hadn't even started. Turns out it was nothing, but we missed the first 10 minutes of class, which was good.

Oh yeah, I'm having this big dilemma. The semi is coming up this Friday but I have no way to get there. My dad doesn't want me driving until my arm is fixed, and I don't want my parents driving me. So that leaves only one option and that is a limo. A limo that I went ahead and booked as of tonight but I don't know if I really want to spend 50 bucks for a 5-minute ride. It's gonna be weird, either spend witlessly or be embarrassed. I don't know, tough choices.

Teresa

Feb 16

Dear Diary,

Well, we had no school yesterday because of Presidents' Day and I was dreading today then because usually when we have a day off the next day is hell. But today went surprisingly fast. My friend Gina is having her birthday in only 2 days!! I hope she gets her license.

This past Saturday I went to the JFK hockey game and then the whole team and me and my dad and other families went over to the captain's house for a postgame dinner, which was fun. Plus there's this one guy on the team who is soooooo hot, so that made it much better. Later on I went to someone else's house, this other guy on the team, and that was a drinking party. Surprisingly, I didn't drink! It was bad though because the guy who is hot was there and he *was* drinking—and then I saw him get in his car to drive. I told him he should just stay or have someone else drive him, but he didn't listen to me. He ended up getting where he was going—but he was lucky!

The semi is coming up this coming weekend but of course I have no date. Oh well, I think I am actually going to go w/Rosie even though she is still with Kevin and I feel weird about that. I have to just deal with it. (Oh yeah, she isn't actually going with Kevin because he already asked someone else before they hooked up.) Anyway, tonite I didn't go out because I was so tired so I just stayed in and watched a movie.

Jake

February 16

I have been a little down lately. Nothing has changed in my dad's condition for a while. And after Valentine's Day, I guess I was just thinking too much. Time is dragging. I want spring to be here now. I am counting the days until lacrosse starts. I am trying to get in shape for it. It is the best game on earth.

Emma

2/16, 8:15 p.m.

I have been so busy since this weekend. I had to babysit all day yesterday and then today we went back to school. I just got off the phone with Cliff. We were just saying again that we had such a nice time this weekend. He *loved* going to dinner and the best part was that he paid for it. I was so shocked but when the check came he took it and just smiled at me. I almost fell over that was so sweet. I also got from him this plastic rose with a teddy bear sitting on top of a huge chocolate kiss holding another plastic rose. Then he gave me this other bear figurine with this love quote on the bottom. Cliff said his mom thought it was cute so she got it for him to give to me. It is really cute, I like it. And the card he gave me was really cute too, I almost started to cry when I first read it. It was just so nice being just the two of us, that was definitely the best part of all. After we ate, we went driving around and ended up at Karen's house for whatever reason. We were all supposed to watch *Armageddon* together, but that never happened. We ended up watching some made-for-TV movie instead. Well, we watched some of it. Then his friends beeped him and we left to go see them. So what happened is we ended up getting into this huge fight about where we were going and how late we were staying and Cliff was saying it was all my fault. He said I made him look stupid in front of his friends. He said I was stubborn and so what was I supposed to say. I was like whatever. I didn't want to fight anymore. Then we made up and everything was ok. I ended up staying with his friends even though I had wanted to leave, but it turned out to be ok to do that. But I did have to leave at 11 so I could get home by 11:30. It was a really good day though. Tonight I am just resting because I have to go to a hockey game tomorrow, Wednesday night. I am really looking forward to it.

Katie

February 17th
@ 6 P.M.

I have had no time this week! Between school, the musical, Community Club, the semiformal, student government, and of course trying to see Brad, I am absolutely going crazy! Anyway, here's what I have been doing day to day this week:

Mon. 2/15: I studied *all* day. It was Presidents' Day so we had off

Tues. 2/16: Dance rehearsal for the musical 3–5
Acting rehearsal a few scenes 5–6
Math tutor 6–7
Meeting over at the senior center 7–8:30
This was soooo nuts I didn't even get to eat until 9!

Wed. 2/17: Acting rehearsal 3–5
Music rehearsal 5–7
Miss Teen County rehearsal 4–9

I had to run between them to go to all of it! I did the pageant because I am one of the student leaders and they wanted someone to represent JFK. It's a lot of fun.

It just feels like this year I am more exhausted than ever. I must stay focused on my longer-term goals.

Baxter

February 17
Well, I got into LIT, otherwise known as Leaders in Training. It's this summer workshop that you have

27

to apply for. I am not even really sure what it is or what it means but Billy and I are both going. I also decided that next year I am going to take AP physics because I really like Ms. Cooney, the woman who teaches it. I think I did really well on the last test. I have decided that maybe I can design cars for a living. That could be cool.

Tonight I watched *Dawson's Creek* and it was great. Jack came out! Everyone knew he was gay anyway. I was glad to see them show that on TV. No one was sure if they would. Of course, my friend Pam was not too happy about it because she thinks Jack is the cutest one on the show. But I think that she only got upset because she's nervous about going for her license tomorrow. She'll do fine, I know it. I go for mine in 8 days. I can't wait, even though I have no car.

Billy

2-18

Ok so tomorrow nite is the semi and my dilemma is solved because Dad gave me driving privileges back. It's going to be really fun and I am even getting a little nervous because it's a big nite. We get all dressed up and then we do the picture thing with our parents. I am going with Ruby Grayson. We never actually even talked to each other and then one day online she was complaining about how she didn't have a date and she might have to go with someone she didn't really want to go with hint, hint, so I figured why not and I asked her. I asked her to go with me just to be nice I guess. I mean, she's a cool person and I think it will be fun. I hope so. I'm wearing a great suit.

Marybeth

February 18th

Well, this a.m. I did some stuff 4 my mom. She wanted me to pick up around the house. She and Dad have been really busy and I think I am trying to be nicer now since we had a talk together about my going out and drinking and all of that. I know I want to be closer to both parents it just takes a little work.

Anyway, after school Emma came by my place and we washed our cars together, which was cool. They looked really cute. And after that, we had dinner b/c Mom came home. Then we went to Cliff's house, and then on to TJ's place. Actually TJ took me back home again. We *FINALLY* hooked up. Let me just say that wow is he a good kisser. Jeez do I want him.

Oh yeah, the other thing that was happening today was that this other guy I like, Matt, IMed me on the computer earlier & it was very weird 4 me 2 hear from him. We haven't talked in like forever.

Tomorrow is the semi!

29

Emma

So this week the coolest things are happening! Okay the first thing is that I won a hockey puck at the hockey game on Wednesday. I was so excited. I mean, what I will do with a puck I have no idea, but it felt cool winning and all. The Bulldogs won too, so now we are on our way to the championships. I have been excited since it happened. We are on our way! The only bad thing was that one of the really good players got hurt and I feel bad because now he can't play in the rest of the games and there is nothing he can do about it. A least he's not a senior so he can get a chance again to play next year. I can't imagine what it would be like if he were a senior that would be so sad for him.

Marybeth and I washed our cars yesterday and had a blast just hanging out. We haven't been doing that so much lately. And of course tonight is the night of the semi and I am excited to go. So is Marybeth. I decided that I wanted to wear my hair different and so I got it done like half up with a bunch of curls on the side. Actually, I was totally lucky and got out of school because it was my job to help set up for the semi. I am like one person in charge on this stupid committee and it was hard. The teachers pick us for the committee so even if we don't want to we have to go. Well, Katie and Sherelle helped out, but it was really hard work. My dress for tonite is this pale pink color it is so pretty. It's short above my knee just a little bit. It just flows and looks nice on me. Cliff told me he's wearing a gray suit and I cannot wait to see him I think we will look good together. I got him a pink rose to put on his jacket and he said my corsage has some pink flowers too so we will look really cute together.

Ok this is the ticket

JOHN F. KENNEDY HIGH SCHOOL

PRESENTS

ROCK AND ROLL

SEMIFORMAL

FEBRUARY 19

7:00 P.M. TO 11:00 P.M.

AT

CLIFFSIDE MANOR

456 KIMBALL ROAD

I just hope everything goes well because I feel like I have worked hard for this moment. After the semiformal wc will probably all head over to Katie's house for a late party. I hope we have fun!!! xoxxxooxx emma

Katie

I have been so involved in the play lately that I haven't had much time for anything else. But it's the semi tonight!

I was so glad this day had finally come and I had been really looking forward to it, but I was so afraid that it wouldn't go smoothly. It would have been hard to mess this up, though, since I spent the last year making preparations! Sherelle, Emma, and I left school at 1 to go pick up balloons. We dropped them off with no major problem and then I went to shower before my hair appt. Then I went from the hair place to the makeup place. For the first time in my life I was ready on time! Brad was shocked! Unfortunately I called Brad around 6 (he was supposed to be here at like 6:15) and he still hadn't showered or shaved or *anything*! Nevertheless, we made it on time after stopping over at Gwen's and then going over to Emma's. We took pictures at both houses and then drove Emma and Cliff and Sherelle and Baxter (they went together) to Cliffside Manor. I was so happy because Brad got along great with everyone—teachers, kids, everyone. We all had a great time at the semi. When I see so many smiles it makes all the time and work and preparation worth it.

A bunch of people came over to my house afterward (most of them just left, actually) and my mom got a TON of food for them to eat. Way too much— she always does that, but she really goes out of her way to make things special. I noticed at one point during my party that Teresa was standing and flirting with Brad, which was really annoying. But then it got so ridiculous it was at the point where it was *FUNNY*! Brad and I were actually laughing about it. I think sometimes Teresa just doesn't know when to stop— she goes that extra mile all the time to get attention. I feel bad but I just feel that she is *really* annoying.

Jake

February 20

Today is my dad's birthday. All I can think about is how he is feeling. I remember when we used to fish and crab together in the bay. I have this cool picture of him smiling with my little sister on the wave runner and now look at him. My dad can't even stand up now. I have never seen him crack a smile like the smile he has in that picture. The only time I even see the beginning of a smile like that now is when I crack a good joke. But I can hardly ever do that.

Yesterday was the semi. It was ok nothing great. I was thinking about going with this girl Bethany who is Aly's cousin but instead I went with a sophomore, this girl Dana Maresco. We actually didn't stay together much because of different friends, but we hooked up.

Kevin

Um ok yeah so yesterday nite was the semi and like it was ok yeah it was pretty cool. We all had fun the only thing was that the DJ there blew big time. Me and Cristina were having a real good time and Cristina looked *REAL* good. And now I have pictures too to keep lookin at her. So as far as me and Rosie go, well, we also hung out a lot during the semi and she danced pretty close to me and sure I feel ok, I'm good w/that. But I still just feel like there is something missing like someone else is always around us like we're never *really* alone, esp. there so that sucked. I just don't get her deal. Um I had to work on Sat. today, which sucked b/c after the semi I was dog tired but oh well. I will prob. go hang at Micky Lazlo's tonite and recover from the semi ha ha.

Billy

2-20

The semi was so great. I was pleasantly surprised how good Ruby looked. Also pleasantly surprised how Ruby acted too because she is usually a quiet person and she was dancing and talking and being outgoing the whole time we were there.

Okay the first thing of the night though is like I said before my dad gave me my driving privileges back again so my parents didn't have to take us. So I picked up Ruby and we did the whole picture thing. It was really nerve-racking with her parents staring me down like, "Is he a good kid?" and "Will he bring her home safe?" I could see that all those feelings seemed to be on their minds. After that I went to Deke's house to take pictures w/my crew. My crew is the best group of guys there are. I am so lucky— Benjamin, Anthony, Lexi, Pete G., Dan, Pat Friday, the 2 Mikes, and Shachter. We have the best time, I mean I know we are immature but that's where the fun is. We have a good time wrestling with each other, playing football, and just overall chilling. All of us were at Deke's house and everyone was there w/their dates. We were all there under the lights, with parents taking pictures and everything. And after that we leave to go to the semi in like a dozen cars and all I can think of is food. Because I am always hungry. The next thing we do is just eat and listen to the music and start dancing around. The energy was really really there. And one of the girls in the group decides right then that she's going to dedicate this song to all us guys as a joke. So 5 of us got onstage and sang w/it. How great.

During the rest of the night I tried to spend as much time as I could w/Ruby. When we danced the slow songs, I think we were getting a little too close though. She was like rubbing my hair and back and I was rubbing her back. Actually now that I think back on the whole thing, it worries me. I like Ruby ok but I don't want to lead her on and she has already called me once since only yesterday. I didn't call back. I think I am gonna keep putting her off. Prob. it's the right thing to do. I don't want her to get hurt in the long run cuz the truth is I have no real or deep feelings for her. I mean I did give her a good-nite kiss at the end of the nite but it didn't mean anything. Am I leading her on again? Who cares.

Marybeth

February 21st

Here is the best newz 4 me: last nite me & Matt (that *HOT* senior who plays hockey) we went to play pool together. I had soooo much fun!!! I think he did too!!! He & I actually went online yesterday for a little bit and he was kinda bored & so was I. Not w/each other but just w/out anything really 2 do. We were talking about this kid we both know who is working at a hotel like carrying luggage or something. Ok so then he was just getting all sarcastic on me and I was a little pissed off. But I still think he's cool of course. I told him he should come over 2 see me but he couldn't just then.

Today I had to work, which was awful, but it was only from 2:10 to 8:00 or so. It was ok. Right now I am on the phone w/this guy Teddy who works w/me. He actually lives like 2 towns away but I see him all the time around here. I even saw him earlier today for like a minute at the mall. I went over there w/Emma to pick out prom dresses. It's like the minute the semi is over that's all we can think about. I really hope I get to do something else w/Matt real soon!

Teresa

Dear Diary,

Oh my God! Gina got her license! Of course she & I have been talking less but I was hoping for her soooo much! She actually got it last Thursday, like right before the semi happened. I am so proud of her b/c she passed absolutely everything! I have to admit, I didn't have much faith in her. I had been driving around w/her once and got so nervous but that's not something I will worry about anymore!

The semi was okay although me and my friend Rosie both went *together* because we were *DATELESS*! But of course the thing is that I am really good friends w/her and she's with Kevin and that makes me feel so weird. It's just so strange! But I was happy b/c at one point my favorite song was on and Kevin grabbed *me* to dance. At least he did once anyway.

I'm coping I guess. I will deal.

I danced pretty much the rest of the nite and the

food was pretty good too. I ate two helpings of baked macaroni and like 10 slices of bread and chicken wings. I have a very big appetite!

Now tonite my brother's ex came over and she fixed my hair and gave me nail tips that look so good. She does that kind of thing. She says I have the most beautiful eyes and she was showing me how to put on this makeup she brought over. She is beautiful too, she has this really long hair that's totally curly but she straightens it for the most part. So after my hair and nails and *makeup* got done, I got picked up by Gina in her *CAR*!!! That was so cool. She was there w/the rest of my girlfriends like Wendy and Steph was there too for a little while. The only thing anyone said that was remotely not good about my new look was that it made me look like kind of a bitch. I guess maybe it does, but people already think that about me sometimes. Anyway, I have gotten dirty looks in the past. But the girls also said I look *OLDER*, and that is definitely a *good* thing. I can't wait to see people's reactions in school. I should wear my favorite outfit too.

Favorite Things Favorite Things

Katie
    Book: Fried Green Tomatoes
    Board game: Life
    TV show: Dawson's Creek
    Movie: Beauty and the Beast

Kevin
    Book· Um I don't READ A lot.
    BoArd gAme· Life
    TV show· Seinfeld, DAwson's CReek
    Movie· Too mAny. Rocky III, Ace
VentuRA, And much moRe

Teresa
    Book: Chicken Soup for the Teenage Soul
    Board game: Candyland
    TV show: Dawson's Creek, of course
    Movie: Titanic (I am a hopeless fan)
and William Shakespeare's Romeo and
Juliet

Baxter
    Book: To Kill a Mockingbird
    Board game: Pictionary
    TV show: Friends

Favorite Things Favorite Things

Movie: <u>Goonies</u>

Marybeth
Book: <u>The Great Gatsby</u> and <u>The Road Home</u>
Board game: I dunno. I like to play cards better.
TV show: <u>That Seventies Show</u> maybe but I don't really watch TV.
Movie: <u>Dumb and Dumber</u>

Billy
Book: <u>The Shining</u>
Board game: Strip poker (not a board game, but fun when you're bored!)
TV show: <u>The Real World</u>
Movie: <u>Armageddon</u>

Emma
Book: <u>Nancy Drew</u> when I was younger
Board game: <u>Guess Who?</u>
TV show: <u>Dawson's Creek</u>, POS, 90210, ER
Movie: <u>Cruel Intentions</u>, <u>Steel Magnolias</u>, <u>My Best Friend's Wedding</u>

Jake
Book: None
Board game: <u>Monopoly</u>
TV show: <u>The Tom Green Show</u>
Movie: <u>Armageddon</u>

Baxter

This has been the best weekend! First of all, the semi on Friday was *GREAT*. I never had so much fun. Sherelle came as my date because Bobby had to do something with his parents. She looked so good. It was a blast. Especially since I spent most of the night dancing with *MEGAN*! And most of the time it was *her* who was asking me to dance. She also gave me a kiss on the cheek before I left!!!!!!!!! We swing danced and that's all she was talking about the next day.

Then on Saturday there was more. Last nite I went to Jessica's Sweet 16 party and once again I spent another night in a row with *MEGAN*! It was so *FANTASTIC*!!!!!!! This has been the best weekend I can remember in a long time.

Saturday and today, Sunday, I'm feeling a little bit sick. My throat is killing me. This morning I went driving with my dad. I am soooooo going to pass on Thursday. It's my birthday and I am so psyched.

The only bad thing that I think has happened this weekend so far is that my grandmother broke her wrist, but she's feeling better. We just celebrated her 90th birthday! My family is so much fun.

Actually there is one other weird thing. Coconut won't eat lately, so we're all keeping an eye on her. I hope my dog's okay. I love her so much.

41

Emma

2/21, 11:00 p.m.

Elizabeth's number/pager 555-0909

This is the number of some girl that Cliff knows and goes to school with. I found it in his jacket. I hate her! She used to go to school with me but freshman year she started going to private school instead. I hate the fact that Cliff is friends with her and there is totally *NO* reason why he is supposed to have her phone number or her beeper number in his pocket. So I just took it when he wasn't looking. If he asks me about it I'll just say I have no idea. And by pasting it into this journal I am absolutely sure he will never find it. I never ever want him to find this!

So the semiformal was a blast! Cliff had a good time even, and that made me so happy. I really thought he was going to hate it and that he would just sit there like facing the wall, but he didn't. He actually danced with me, which is saying a lot since he like *NEVER* dances! His friend from school was there and so they hung out together some too. It was good that they each had someone to talk to.

Kevin

Ok I'm sick I don't feel good still. Sunday when I woke up I drank a lot of juice but that didn't help much & I rested too!! I did go out for ice cream with Micky, me, Betsy & Cristina but today I was feelin worse again. So um there's this thing that happened the other nite like my friend Randi is bitching to me about it this stupid stupid thing. Ok so May has this party and it was about to be all busted up and so people ran like everywhere & cops were like all around. I was gone at the time & when I got back I had people all in my car so no more could fit in it. So then Randi is there and she sees my car and she tries to get in so as not to get in trouble. Then I'm like get out there's no room here in the front and now we are fighting because she was forcing her way into the car & I wouldn't let her. Anyway when I got home I wrote her this e-mail b/c I was so pissed.

I'm tryin to be civil here and work through something with you but that just doesn't work I guess unless you talk to me in return and for whatever reason you won't do that. If you seriously don't value my friend-ship then just say so & I will give it up.
Someone told me that they saw you & you were in trouble & about to be arrested and so

then you hoped I would put you in my car so
you could get out of trouble. But then I had
like 5 people in my car already seriously it
was jammed in tight with me, Micky Lazlo,
Geffen, Manny R., and Jacob. Ok so if there
was more room you know I would have let you in
but I said like 10 times there was no room!!!
Even if you had been able to squeeze in (which
you couldn't) then a cop probably would have
seen us & then he would have busted *all of us*
and then where would we be I don't know why
you just couldn't shut the fucking door & go.

One of your responsibilities when you go to
a party is to know that you might get caught &
you told me that if you had been the one dri-
vin you would have done different and I just
wanna know how & what. Now I would be mad if a
friend left me I would but the other thing
here is that a friend would try to understand
& know that I did everything in my power to
deal w/the situation as it was. But no you
can't do that apparently. Since the other nite
you are just walkin around w/this total bitchy
attitude whether I offend you by pointing that
out or not I don't care b/c that's what it
was—bitchy. So if you actually choose to ignore me and keep ignoring me fine whatever for
you it was real nice knowing you & losing you
over some petty little thing.

So after the e-mail I get a call from Randi and she
was still a *TOTAL BITCH* to me. She was like saying

how she doesn't even care, how she is "over" it, and how I have no right to lecture her b/c I am the one who has the problem & that I ended up talking shit about her to everyone (which is *NOT* true). She said that I shouldn't expect anything to be the same & that it was a real wake-up call to her about what I am *really* all about and I mean what the fuck is that? I don't see how I always end up the bad person here I mean I would admit if I was wrong and *I WASN'T*.

Jake

February 22

I have work to catch up on so I haven't been going out much.

I did hear about this stupid stuff at some party over the weekend. I wasn't there though. What I heard happened was that this friend of mine Randi was trying to get away from the cops at some party on the other side of town. Kevin was there. Of course she went to him and tried to get in his car. Kevin's car was packed so he couldn't take her. From what I hear he was not nice and could have been nicer. Also he could have told her he had no room and then just smoothed things out. The problem was that Kevin got real pissed and in one of his moods as usual. I heard he cursed her and slammed the door and then she got real pissed. I am not sure who was wrong but it definitely sounded like Kevin should have been nicer. I also heard that now they are not speaking.

Baxter

February 22

I just got off the phone with Emma and she says that she heard that Kevin almost got into a screaming fight with this girl Randi from our class. It was at some party that of course I was not invited to go to. The cops were there at some point.

Em says that Kevin was calling Randi names for no reason and that she was hysterical. And it was all because he would not give her a ride home from the party. I can't believe it. Why couldn't he just give her a ride home?

Coconut still won't eat food. I am more worried. I think we should take her to the vet one more time.

Katie

February 22
@ 10 P.M.

I can't believe the amount of activity that is going on around me. I am soooo tired right now! It has been the longest weekend! Of course my party after the semi was good, I said that, and the next day we went to take breakfast to feed the homeless and we had food, some books, and a few clothes. There weren't many people there, but we cooked for ourselves. It is through Community Club that we do it and it's the funniest thing because there are the most unexpected kids who have joined up since the beginning of the year. It seems like this year the kids in Community Club are the ones who drink and smoke pot on Saturday nights. Then they come to feed the homeless? It is shocking, but it's still nice to see everyone bonding together and getting involved. That's what matters—participation. It's like how I feel about planning ahead and making goals; I just don't understand why people make excuses about participation!

We had a weekend play practice too and I danced for five hours. We're all pulling together as a cast now, and I really think it will turn out to be an awesome production. The set is unbelievable too. When I am not dancing and on break, I take turns with this guy Deke (he's on the football team with Billy) and we paint the set. No one trusts my paint job, though, I guess, because Mr. Remmers puts down tape strips to make sure I paint in between all the lines! I was not amused.

Anyway, after dancing, I ran home and went to this practice for the Miss Teen County, this pageant that I am sort of helping out at. It's actually a prelim. for the Miss America Pageant, and I'm just a student rep there because they have student teen reps from all the local schools. Well, I got to meet the girl who won it last year and believe it or not she went to Stanford—like I will maybe? Looks like I have another good connection for when I apply soon! I need all the help I can get since it is so hard to get in anywhere. She said she would help me in anything that I needed. Yeah! After the pageant ended I helped clean up too and then Brad picked me up. I was starving again! I am just not eating at regular times these days. I am just exhausted—but I love having all this stuff going on at once!!!!!

Billy

2-22

Nothing really going on at school. Nothing really going on, period. It's just the same old ritual where you go and sit there, all day, get homework, take a quiz or a test or something like that, and then just sit there more. Blah blah blah. Yeah, well, I have to go watch *RAW*. This wrestling shit is so good. Later.

Marybeth

February 22nd

I wuz really bored in school like a wk ago and now it is better *SO* much btr! I wrote this good essay a few days ago for English class after reading *Death of a Salesman,* which was a good book, play. In the book, Willy Loman is struggling to accept the man he has become. He wants to be not just liked, but well liked. He wants a house but then also an extra guest house for his sons to come & visit. But none of his dreams of life ever came true—they were all just dreams. He lost this battle against his own self. I wonder how true that is for everyone 2 some degree—r we all like Willy Loman in some way?

So his family is there 4 him, and his friends 2, but Willy still cannot get it together on his own. His wife Linda makes all these excuses for him but he never takes responsibility for reality. He never deals with the way things really r around him. He should just be happy w/what he has, but that is not possible and he always looks 4 more. It was such a true story. I really think that's how life is for people, a lot of peeps actually! It is *HARD* to accept the way stuff turns out sometimes but the thing is that we have to deal with reality & not some crazy dream. But life is just what it is. I think sometimes when I am alone like now what do I really want and what do I dream? I guess I just will always be the kind of person who takes it like it comes.

Oh well, that's my philosophy for 2day. G'nite!

I get my license in 57 days!!!!

Teresa

Feb 23

Dear Diary,

I am sooooo happy that Gina has her license! She has been driving me like all over the place it's soooo awesome! We even drove past Jesse's house (from hockey, etc.) and we beeped like 6 times as we went past! Then of course we went for food!

I can't do without *FOOD*! Gotta have that.

Tonite my dad and I had a very long talk about how things are going lately. It seems like ever since my Sweet 16 this year he is just preoccupied with what is going on in our life. First of all, he hates so much not being able to live with me. I understand, but I refuse to move out of my house or away from Mom so that won't happen. Also, he is getting very upset as of late about me being out so much. Because my two best girlfriends now are driving that means that he won't have to drive me around anymore. Now he won't see me much, or that's what he's worried about happening. He is very upset about this. I don't know what to tell him. He just has to live with it I guess. I'm still coping!

I Love You, Daddy

When I was a little girl you would hold me tight
And make sure that no matter what things went right.
And when Mommy and you would sometimes fight
You were always there to hug me good night.
Now I am older and time is passing on
And the little girl you loved has moved on.
I love you, Daddy, my heart says so
But I have a life to live and places to go.
I know I am passing through many doors

But no matter how far I leave, my heart is yours.
You worry about where I am going and what I do
You worry that growing up takes me away from you.
But I am here to say that I will always be your T.
Our special tie won't be broken by me.
—T. J. F., 2/23

Emma

2/23, 8:35 p.m.

This past week is like some blur I think. Of course the semiformal was really a lot of fun but the rest of the weekend was a little rough. I went to feed the homeless with Katie actually, and I couldn't even keep my eyes open. I just want to sleep all the time for some reason. And then Sunday and Monday were not so good either. And today was a really bad day for me because I just did not feel well. And it is only Tuesday so I had better feel better soon. I had SAT class again. I also had to go to this wake. My friend Sam's mom died. Sam plays hockey and he and I have become semiclose this year so I felt like I really should go and be there for him. This poor kid has been through a really awful fall and spring he is upset like all the time. I started to cry as soon as I walked into the room where they had the wake. His dad came right over to me though and was so nice. I feel so bad for Sam. But I know he will be strong and he will get through this somehow. He has to stay strong for his family. And we also have a hockey game tomorrow. I don't know if he will be there or not but the team totally wants to win just for Sam and his whole family. I hope we win.

Baxter

February 23

The two worst things that could possibly happen happened today. First thing is that Britney twisted her ankle working on her new video. Can you believe that? Isn't that terrible for her? Also Megan asked me for a ride in my car today. So then I will not be alone with Jessica in my car on Thursday so no moves will be made. That *SUCKS*!!!!!! I keep going back and forth between those two.

School's great in spite of everything else happening. Community Club is almost over and that can't come soon enough, right? I have been avoiding *THE COW* Miss Shapiro for months. Now I won't have to do that.

Chem and physics are suddenly ok. I get them. And now I think I have definitely decided that what I want to do is to design cars. Plus I get my own license in 2 days. *I CAN'T WAIT*! I am so so so so so going to pass.

Billy

Overall, school is so stupid. Same ol' same ol'. We had a test in math today on probability. It was pretty easy but still. I am doing well in that class thank God. Going from a B– to an A–. Nothing else really happening except after school we had play practice for *The Boy Friend*. It is fun but it is also really strenuous. But it's cool to be with good friends like Deke and Katie and working on theater. I like that. I hope that the show goes well. I am crossing my fingers.

The only bad thing I forgot to mention is that my physical therapist says my arm is still not great. He thinks I am trying to use it too much. Maybe I am. I was even trying to figure out how I could play lacrosse next week but I guess not for now. Have to sit this one out for another week or so. I'll make it I hope. I miss the team.

Jake

February 24

I have decided that lacrosse is the best. I love it so much because it is always moving. Always moving. There is hitting and talent involved, but anyone can do it. You just get caught up in it. I started playing when I was in 6th grade and never stopped. I just got attached to it since it's the best game on earth. And our team is doing well too. Of course I feel bad for Billy, who has been on the bench a lot of the season so far, but we are just getting started. He'll come back. We have lacrosse practices and games on Saturdays from now on until the end of the season. My coach is already a little annoyed because I have to miss 2 practices due to work.

At home, Dad is not so good, but I am used to it by now.

Marybeth

February 25th

Only like a month and a half now until I get my license!!!! Oh God I was in this small accident today with my friend she was driving and hit a car. . . . She didn't see it. . . . It really sucked and I feel so awful for her we r all ok tho. Today in school there were a bunch of people absent. Everyone seems to be coming down with something. Probably the flu. 95 kids were out of school yesterday but even more were out today. Oh well, at least I am healthy (knock on wood). Today I tried to go running, but it was so damn cold. I didn't make it far b/c my asthma started ↑. And I am really tired tonight for some other reason. I think I will go 2 bed early. . . . BTW tomorrow is the ice-hockey game & if JFK wins we get the cup or something.

Emma says it's a big deal. I'm going to go, but only to watch Matt play. I still like him, I admit it. I can't let myself fall for him this time but it is so hard not 2 b/c he is such a hottie! Oh well. I just hate guys sometimes.

What's Attractive To Me

<u>Kevin:</u>

Long straight hair, short, curly, whatever . . . um A pretty face not too much makeup at all. She has to have a good sense of style that is like mine And like a lot in common with me. It is soo A plus when we get along great. They don't have to be tall or short just not too short gets tuff to kneel w/them on tippy toes. They don't have to be big huge boobs truthfully too big gets Annoying And nasty I think. Just something nice & I love A nice round plump (LOL) ass ohh man but I don't want A bulimic chic ok someone who is skinny but not too skinny with some love handles he he he.

<u>Katie:</u>

Definitely a natural intelligence is the most attractive quality in a person, and a great sense of humor of course. I really think that a sense of humor is the key factor that makes someone want to be around others.

What's Attractive To Me

Marybeth:

It depends. . . . Sometimes nice eyes . . . and someone has to be funny if they can do that. . . . I'm all urs. . . . I'm not too picky. . . . Ok like they can't be couch potatoes r n e thing. . . . I hate guys that think they r hard asses = TURNOFF.

Billy:

Looks first. Not drop-dead gorgeous but a good-looking girl. However, the most important thing is personality. When a girl is sweet and outgoing, that is key.

Baxter:

What is attractive to me is people who don't get freaked out. There is nothing worse than someone who will change their personality because they need to look good for some other people. I don't like people who can't laugh. I do like when someone feels comfortable with who they are. That is attractive.

What's Attractive To Me

Teresa:

My standards are so high!!! Oh gosh it takes a lot for me to be attracted to someone. First thing . . . I notice things like haircuts, and teeth and clothing. I'm more attracted to brunettes, but that's just coincidence, not personal preference. If a guy has a nice tan, that always helps! I like good teeth, and good hygiene of course. I like guys who dress like really nice like GAP, Structure, Abercrombie & Fitch, things like that. Not so much preppy, just very nice like khakis and nice shirts. I love nice-colored eyes and I am absolutely obsessed with tall guys . . . the taller the better! Muscles aren't that important to me, but at the same time, I do NOT want a scrawny guy. As far as social stuff, he can drink but not too much, only once in a while. I do not want a party animal and not someone who is obsessed with his friends. He has to be really sensitive but not like

58

What's Attractive To Me

to the point where he mauls me and yearns for love. Just someone who doesn't have an ego problem. Brains are essential—he MUST be smart and know where he's going or have some sort of goals. So with these requirements, it's probably clear why I don't have a boyfriend!

Jake:

Personality is definitely a plus. And a big chest.

Emma:

I used to like those noodie-type people with thick chains and stuff I dunno why. I just did. And of course I like guys who like to dance. What is really really attractive now to me is just someone who is nice and who I can talk to about anything. A good listener is like the best thing. Cliff is a good listener and he buys me flowers too.

Baxter

February 25

Well, today is my birthday and *I GOT MY LICENSE*!!!

It is so great. The best thing is that my parents surprised me with a car! Okay, let me start from the beginning. I passed everything, but the driving instructor guy was a real jerk. He said I performed adequately and he didn't even congratulate me. Then I got $2\frac{1}{2}$ hours to spend in the DMV because they lost all my paperwork for some reason.

So finally I got it later and on the way home when my driveway came into view I saw something sitting there. It was a red car with a giant bow and balloons on it. *I FLIPPED OUT.* I was so happy.

Now I am going to dinner with Emma, Marybeth, and Cliff. It was really nice of them to plan this.

Emma

2/25, 11:40 p.m.

Happy birthday to Baxter!

Today was his special day and he got his license and his parents even got him a CAR! He was so excited. His test was at noon and he said he was going to take it and then come back to study for his physics test. Well, at 2:15, I walked by and he wasn't there and didn't beep me. I was getting nervous because I thought what if something happened and he failed? Well, it turns out that he got stuck at the DMV for like 2 hours because they lost his papers or something. I had a feeling that he would pass though and that his parents would get him a car. I just had that feeling. I mean they got one for his older brother Jerry so I knew they would have to get one for him. Baxter works so hard in school and his parents are rewarding him, which is good. He really deserves this. Marybeth, Cliff, and I went over to see the car right away. It's red and he looks really cute in the driver's seat.

After we looked at the car, we all went out for dinner for his birthday. We took him for Mexican because that's what he wanted to eat. I had some nachos and they were really good. We told him we were going to sing to him in the restaurant but then he said no way. But the truth was that Marybeth went to the bathroom and told the waitress about it being Baxter's birthday. She came out with this huge slab of mousse cake covered with chocolate shavings and with one candle in it. It looked so cool! The three waiters and waitresses sang to him and his face turned all red! It was funny. I am sure he was happy that we took him out or at least I hope so. It is one of his favorite restaurants. So that made it better.

Jake

February 26

School is the same old boring sh*t. I guess I am getting better grades now. Some of my teachers are starting to piss me off more like my English teacher and my history teacher but who cares hopefully I won't have to deal with them again next year.

Well, everyone is gettin their licenses and I want mine. Weekends are starting to get more fun because now people actually go out and I have been to at least one party a weekend. Of course I still can't wait for lacrosse and my love life still sux. Yeah, there are hookups but I would like to get kind of steady with one. Other than that the hookups are nice. No Community Club bullshit for me. No SAT prepping either because I never took the class but I do a little work by myself at home. I hope I do good but I am not sure what is going to happen. How much do I care?

Katie

February 26
@ 9:35 P.M.

Okay, it's now Friday of a really crazy week. I swear that everything just gets worse & worse as the play gets closer. Plus there's SATs coming up soon and so I have been trying to prepare for that with my tutor. The play is actually only *two weeks* away! Wow, is that ever nerve-racking. I am trying to keep it all in perspective of course.

The most unbelievable thing that has happened is that Rachel Ross and I are getting along really well. We realize that as the 2 female leads in this production we have to get along or else! We have to pull this one off. Okay, it's not like we hang out on weekends, but we are at least civil to each other. Anything is an improvement over the fall, when we were competing in tennis, right?

Some other big things are going on too. This past week part of my class had like a field trip to this art museum. It was an adjunct activity to our English class. We didn't really do much there except talk a lot so it ended up being a very good opportunity to bond with some people. Of course Gwen and I were together. We were actually spending a little time with this girl we were both friends with in grammar school. Anyway, she is having some serious issues about drugs. We think she's taking some kind of stimulants or something. It's bad. I hate to see someone I care about destroying herself a little bit by bit. I hope she can get better and deal with her issues.

Brad says he never sees me. I guess that's how it has to be for now!

Kevin

2/26

I am getting sicker and sicker and it kills me I am not goin out and no one ever sees me I feel like shit! I had to work of course tonite and that sucked too. Me and Rosie are def. still talking, which is cool I really like her a lot. Um school on the other hand has been freakin boring same thing as usual and I'm out. Ta ta

Billy

2-26

Let it be, oh let it be, just let it be, oh let it be
whisper words of wisdom, let it be

This is def. my newfound fave lyric. Just go with the tide. There is so much happening at school lately and I just want to go with the flow. If something stressful springs up, I need to evaluate the importance of a given situation and figure out whether I need to let it be or to go full steam ahead at the problem.

I just got off the phone w/Baxter. I was wishing him a happy b-day. He got a car and was psyched. I guess I'm happy for him.

Teresa

Feb 26

Dear Diary,

I went this week to an art museum with my English class. Katie was there too. It was so boring. I can't even really remember what we saw at the museum. Isn't that terrible? So anyway me and Gina stayed together the entire time because *WE WERE SO BORED!* We would look at these portraits of colonial people and I got this weird heavy and creepy feeling. It's hard to explain how being bored can make you so totally tired. I would sit down to take a short break and then it was like I couldn't even get up.

Then we went to lunch, which was very good since as usual—I was absolutely starving! We all ran into this KFC and when we were in there we saw this group of hot guys outside across the street. So, needless to say, me and Gina and this other girl just about sprinted out the door. Of course they were gone by the time we got there.

Marybeth

February 27th

Am I right side up or am I upside down
And is this real or am I dreaming?
—DMB

Well, this day was great until about 5 minutes ago. Aside from school and work the best part was I found out my sister Kyra got engaged! I was so happy. I still am. And tonight I went out with my friend May. We went & got something to eat and then came home & hung out at my house. Usually everyone goes 2 play pool at May's b/c her parents are never around, but tonite we wanted to do something different. It was me, May, her bf Damon, and this kid Luther. Damon and Luther had beer in May's car. When Luther was getting ready to take off, he said he wanted to get his beer out of May's car and so he went to do that. Well, my mom saw him. And then my dad came downstairs and called me to tell me it was late and everyone better go right now.

So then I said goodbye and I ran upstairs to go hide in my room. And then when everyone had gone, my mom came in and she was *SCREAMING*. She screamed that she saw the beer that Luther had taken out of the back of the car that I had been driving in. Now she said she is beyond furious with me and that I am pretty much done for. This definitely sucks. Why is she being this way? Why can't she trust me? Didn't we already have this conversation like 100 times?

I don't know what I am going to do, or what I can even say. She thinks I was drinking and of course I wasn't. I mean, the other day when I was in that car accident with Pam, she got worried on me too. And now this. She prob. won't let me out of the house for like a really long time.

I am screwed.

Emma

Driving has been going really well so far. I guess. There sure are some stupid people on the road and that makes me not want to drive. And something freaky happened to Marybeth, who was in the car with Pam driving the other day and was in a freaky car accident. You have to be so careful. Here is what happened. Pam was in her parents' car and she really ruined it. She hit some lady because she wasn't paying attention. It really was *her* fault unfortunately. I mean she's only had her license for like a week or so. And now she is like *REALLY* afraid to drive or even get in a car. The lady she hit was really a bitch too I guess. Like she was yelling at Pam and of course Pam was in tears already as it was, and the lady didn't make it any better. Pam says her dad is wicked mad about the whole thing. Her parents were in California when it happened. It was just a big huge mess and it was too bad that it happened to Pam of all people. Marybeth was pretty upset too because she thought she should have been able to say something to Pam before the accident happened. But she didn't. I am just so glad that Pam wasn't all alone when the whole thing happened. Of course all of this makes me not want to drive. I know I can't be thinking like this! Sherelle gets her license soon so maybe she can sometimes drive me places like I drive her places.

Things with me and Cliff are good. We really look cute together I think.

Teresa

Feb 27

Dear Diary,
Hey! This week I had to go to this second honor society presentation for my town (since I live in the next town over from everyone else). So all I needed to do was stand up there and accept the award, or so I thought. It ended up that they shoved this microphone in my face and I had to say things about the whole honors program and I am sure I sounded really dumb. But I felt proud to be recognized like that for all the hard work I have done and am doing.

So I am leaving in a few minutes to go to see Jaclyn at college! I said I would be going back about now to see Jaclyn with my pal Wendy and *I AM*! I know that I will get drunk and I want Wendy there to be my guardian angel and have a lot of laughs too. The only problem w/Wendy is that she has a boyfriend now and therefore she is not as excited as me about our little excursion. Like tonite I totally plan on hooking up and she obviously isn't. But I am sure she will manage to have fun in some other way—she always does!

Baxter

February 28

I love my new car. It's a used Toyota Corolla and it's 2-door with pop-up headlights. The only thing is that the lights don't work. So I can't drive at night. Yet.

I LOVE MY PARENTS.

After I passed my driving test, I went back to school to pick up Megan but she already left. I had a physics test too but I had to retake it because I was late. The stupid DMV was the one that made me late. But everything was okay because Marybeth and Emma came over to see the car and then took me to dinner. That was so nice.

I think I did okay on the retake of the physics test the next day. It was tricky but I was prepared. Then Friday night was my family party, which was fun.

I LOVE MY PARENTS!

Kevin

2/28

Friday was ghetto in school really nothing going on at all. At nite I worked from 5:40 to 8:00 or so b/c it was my new schedule. So then b/c of that I missed hanging out w/Jonny & Jake all b/c of some misunderstanding. I just seem to be on a dif. wavelength than those guys these days. I dunno what is goin on.

So instead I hung out w/Rosie and Lazlo and his woman at her house. I dropped over b/c Baxter had this family party that he invited me to go to but I only stayed for like half an hour or so. Then Sat. I went to work again and that was like mad stupid b/c I was sooooo sick afterward. I slept a lot but I can't shake it. I went to bed. All I feel like doing is sleepin . . . ta ta.

Jake

February 28

I can't believe it is almost March. I feel like I am so busy and time is going pretty fast. I am not that tired though, which is good. I can keep working too.

I had sort of a bad episode at work recently. Well, one day at work this week my boss promised me a raise. Then he changed his mind or something and then he said he couldn't give it to me then. So I got upset because I needed the money because I pay for everything I want for myself now. I am not used to it. So I started to tear up a little because all I could think about is my dad and what is happening with him. So my boss took me into a conference room and told me he would see what he could do.

Katie

February 28
@ 9:30 P.M.

It's Sunday and I am trying to catch up on some work. Baxter celebrated his birthday this weekend, which was great. He got his license and I am so happy for him.

Yesterday I had a flower sale for Madrigals, my singing group at school. We have no money in the budget but we need some! Of course I also had rehearsals for *The Boy Friend*. I am getting good at the dance numbers but I still cannot believe that the production is only a few weeks away—11 days until the dress rehearsal, to be exact. Time goes by so fast! I have so much to do! I really should go call Brad but I am so tired I think I will go to bed right now.

Emma

2/28, 3:30 p.m.

Today I went shopping with my mom for prom dresses. I looked around a little last weekend, but not with Mom. Actually at 4:40 I need to get over to our church too because the youth minister there is going on this long trip and so everyone thought it would be a good idea to have a surprise party for her. I think that is so funny since yesterday was the day I had a

71

surprise party for my cousin Edie, who was *definitely* surprised. It was cool to see the look on Edie's face even though she was really pissed off a little because she wasn't wearing any makeup!

It is raining outside right now. I really wish it would stop. I hate the rain. I hate driving in the rain. I have to go get dressed for church. I haven't been in 2 weeks so I should make a little effort.

My Religion My Religion

Katie:

My family goes to church together. I sing in choir and I serve on the volunteer committee at my parish. I am also a peer counselor and head of Community Club, which isn't a direct part of the church, but it serves a greater good like church. That's what is important to me.

Billy:

I am really skeptical about all kinds of religion. 95% of the people in this world believe religion blindly whether they are Christian, Jew, Muslim, or whatever and ask no questions at all. Religion is like this controversial truth. I think it is separating us when what we need is to be united.

Marybeth:

It is good 4 me when I am feeling not 2 good. Here's a little prayer my mom gave to me: <u>Step by step, prayer by prayer, the Lord will always get you there.</u>

My Religion My Religion

Baxter:
I believe in God and go to church with my parents every Sunday.

Teresa:
I want to always be very spiritual no matter what. There is this poem in <u>Chicken</u> <u>Soup</u> <u>for</u> <u>the</u> <u>Teenage</u> <u>Soul</u> II called "Give Random Acts of Kindness a Try!" by Melissa Broeckelman. It is sooooo cool because it mainly says the most important thing to do is to just give your joy to others in a smile or with a cheerful word. That is so me. It says: "We're only given a short time to spread some cheer before we die, / So why not give random acts of kindness a try?"

Jake:
How am I supposed to follow any religion when my dad is so sick?

My Religion My Religion

Emma:

I believe in God. That's it pretty much. I like volunteering for Community Club because it is about the same stuff church is about.

Kevin:

I believe in God And heAven And All thAt but I just don't understand so mAny things About how religion works in this world. I don't like being forced to go to church where I hAve to conform to someone else's interpretAtion of the Bible or whAtever. Why does A priest or some other religious person hAve the right to chAnge words thAt were written like so long Ago? I meAn these priests hAve no right. They weren't there with Jesus or Anything. And AnywAy how cAn our God sit bAck And wAtch All of the bAd thAt's going on? How cAn he not step in And fight for whAt is right? Why is there suffering?

Billy

Well, it's Monday now. The weekend passed like it always does—too quickly.

Friday the practice for the play was canceled, at least for me. That was good as it always is. A little more time to rest. So on Friday nite me, Deke, Anthony, Roger, and Lexi were out and about at the mall. We are now calling ourselves the horde. We were sick of calling ourselves the crew so we came up w/that. It's my little gang I guess you could say.

On Saturday, I had a dance rehearsal for *The Boy Friend* from 1 to 5 or so. Well, it sounds like a long time but the truth is that I am not in that many scenes so basically I just sit around and watch Katie and the rest do all the real work. Later on Sat. nite I went to this other drinking party. It was over at Roger's place, with mad people there. Finally some of the seniors at JFK went and it was so happening. I was psyched to be there. Ok, so it was actually a sausage party, which means ha ha there weren't so many girls there but it was still pretty great. We had beer, we told jokes, we fucked around and had a great time. It was great.

On Sunday—yesterday—I caught up on my homework and tonite, Monday, I get to see *RAW*. It's on *every* Monday. I love it. It is a ritual thing for me. For whatever reason I adore the WWF!

Kevin

3/1

So there I am lying in bed today and all I can think is that I feel sicker than I even was before. I slept the whole morning like until 8 and I got to school late. I mean today was a bit better but I was actually just as sick and didn't know that. I went to school & worked basically all day after school and speaking of school, I did not see Rosie around. I don't know what is up, but I'll deal I guess. I do like Rosie. I wish she knew how much I like her. I also wish I had blown off school today. Next time ta ta.

Teresa

Mar 1

Dear Diary,

Well, I didn't go to school today but I had a great time visiting w/Jaclyn. College is great! Okay, here's what happened—there is *SO MUCH* to tell.

We got there at like 2:30. Like the minute we got there the cool guys from across the hall from Jaclyn weren't there. The coolest one, Charles, was at work. So after we got settled in for the weekend, we took a ride and went to eat at a really good restaurant just off campus. After we finished eating, we went back to Jaclyn's room. Still no one was home so we were kinda bored for a little bit. Neither me nor Wendy wanted to see anything in particular so we just sat around and talked.

Finally, around dinnertime we decided to go to the campus social center and buy some drinks to mix with vodka and whiskey. While we walked around we also went into a Wendy's (ha ha!) and ate. Wendy loves Wendy's, naturally. It was weird. While we were eating dinner I kept having this very strange feeling in my stomach, like I was really nervous about something, but I had no clue about what. And then what was really strange was that Wendy said she had the same exact feeling as me.

Now the rest of the night is like a total blur. But I remember a little bit here and there: We went back to Jaclyn's and all these people showed up. People were coming over there because we were all going to a frat party together later on. So anyway, 2 guys show up, Will and Dean, claiming to be half brothers. They started out being really cool but my perception of them changed. So me & Wendy start drinking— Jaclyn mixed us vodka, Sprite, and fruit punch. It was really really good. Even Wendy, who *HATES* the taste of alcohol, had 3 drinks. She was loving it.

Okay, now at this point we were beginning to get a little bit drunk. Finally! The neighbor from across the hall came over. Now last time I was away at Jaclyn's, Charles and I totally hit it off. He is so funny and an overall great guy so I was excited to see him again. Unfortunately, right at this same time, Will and

Dean were starting to piss me off. They were drunk assholes.

Eventually we made it over to the frat party, where Jaclyn hooked up with her bf. I met some other guys there too like this one hot guy Dan and some other people. And after talking to everyone for a while, I found out that we all had mutual friends. That was cool. So we're talking about all these random people and by now I am feeling very drunk. To be truthful, I am not even sure I remember how we got to the frat party but there we were and I was laughing about it. I was there dancing with Charles of course, he asked me. And then he and I started hooking up. It was so great. And Wendy has a bf but she was still dancing and having a fun time.

Needless to say we all got home very very late and had way too much fun for one night! We got everyone's # so we can keep in touch. What a stay!

Marybeth

March 2nd

Well, my sister Kyra came home and I am so happy 4 her. I cannot believe she is really getting married. Wow. I took a nap today after school and it was so refreshing. I was thinking about everything that has been happening, which is so much!

This Friday, I am going snowboarding and I can't wait.

Haven't gotten an e-mail back from Matt. Oh well.

Mom and Dad are still pissed. This is the worst time ever. I really wonder what's going to change here? I want them to trust me.

Baxter

March 2

Well, nothing has changed. I got a bad grade on that physics test from the other day, and I really thought I had done well! How is that possible, I want to know. I got a C+. I know it's actually the average grade but that's not what I want to be. I would like to be above average. At least I got Student of the Month for Academics for Social Studies. That's something good.

I had like 10 people over on Saturday for my birthday. That was fun. We all watched *There's Something About Mary*. That movie was not as funny as I thought but we were laughing the whole time. All day Saturday I spent in my new car. I took my buddy Derek out for a really long ride everywhere. That was cool. I felt so important being able to drive. I can't explain it.

Emma was in such a weird mood today. She just seemed snotty to me. I don't know what was really going on. I have to ask her about it.

Jake

March 3

Sometimes dealing with all these doctors gets my dad crazy. He had to go back to the hospital for more tests yesterday. I hope he will be fine. The other night I was watching *Touched by an Angel* with him and at the end of this episode there was a son talking to his father about how sorry he was for everything and how he is going to miss him. And at that point in the show I just looked in the mirror in my dad's room and I saw him. He was starting to cry and I left the room. I had to leave so I could go into my room to cry by myself.

Emma

3/3, 4:40 p.m.

Yeah, I got a prom dress! My mom almost started crying when she saw it on because it was so pretty! It is really pretty and I really love it. I tried on like 10 dresses but then I finally found the right one I wanted. It is pink and it looks perfect. The top has little flowers embroidered or something on top and then there is this satin sash and a bow right below my chest. It is just so pretty and I think that Cliff will love it even more than I do. And the best part is that it was already on sale *plus* I got a 30% discount on top of that. My shoes are probably going to cost more than my dress did.

I am so excited and I can't wait for the prom. I know it is like months away but I am still excited. The only problem is that because Cliff goes to another school he has a separate prom and unfortunately the 2 proms are on the same nite. It sucks. Katie just told me about it. I called Cliff right away and was like, "What are we going to do?" and he said that he doesn't want to go to his stupid prom anyway so he says we can go to the JFK prom instead. Of course this is so far away from now, but I like planning this stuff way in advance. I think Cliff will definitely have fun though since he had so much fun at the semi a week or so ago.

There is some bad news coming my way in chem. I can tell that I am getting a progress report that says my grades are slipping. It's all because of one quiz, one stupid quiz, and my teacher knows that. Like 8 people in class got zeros and so everyone's average went down. I have never gotten a warning before and now Mr. MacTaggart is going to give me one. I may tell my mom before it comes home so she won't be pissed.

The only thing that really stinks is that my grade is now officially a D+ so in order to bring up my grade to a B, I have to bust my butt. I will not get lower than a B on my report card there is NO way that is happening.

Why is school still so boring or is there just something wrong with me? Boring as hell and I am seriously gonna go nuts at school. Anyway I'm happy and chilling out b/c this week I had a day or so off from work. Oh yeah, this Friday me, Marybeth, Jake, and Cristina are cutting school and going snowboarding. We got our rental snowboards and I am so *STOKED*!

On the other side of life and how I am feeling I was watching TV the other day and started thinking about Jake's dad. There was this show on PBS that showed different patients with the same problem that Jake's dad has. It scares me so much there were a lot of people in the segment and almost no one could really function. There was also this part about committing suicide with Dr. Kevorkian. I don't get it. I was thinking about how much Jake must be dealing with right now and for the last couple of years. Of course I don't know how he does it, how he deals with all the sadness or the stress. I don't know how Jake feels about anything. I think he is overwhelmed. It is all so sad. I love him so much. He is really like a brother to me.

Billy

Blah blah blah same old shit as usual. The constant drag of school is dragging me with it. Then we have play practice from 3 to 5 and then from 5 to 6 a dinner break and then we go back and rehearse more from 6 to 8. What a great time to relax—only a friggin hour. Oh well . . . that's life. At least my arm is better. The therapy has been working. I am all set for lacrosse.

Of course lacrosse is just another thing that will screw me up. I have lacrosse practice on Mar. 8 and that's a few days before opening nite of the show. I don't know what I should do. Maybe I should go to practice and skip the 3 to 5 practice and just go to the 6 to 8 practice and skip dinner too. I mean I like the play but I don't really care that much, but I cannot let all of my friends down, especially Katie b/c she has been so into the whole thing. I have to try my best and hope that the play goes well. So far though everything has just been hectic. All day I am out and I don't get home until like 9 p.m. and I rarely get much sleep due to homework. This definitely sux.

Katie

March 4
@ 10 P.M.

Play rehearsals and schoolwork and Community Club and everything have just been *NUTS*! Basically, my life is pretty mundane. I mean, I am really busy but the truth is that every day is repetitive. Essentially it has been rehearsal from 3 to 5 every day. And now I have strep throat so I can't sing very well. I was sitting in rehearsal tonight and I felt a little down because of the role I have. Mr. Remmers, our drama coach, promised I had an important part but the truth is that Mme. Dubonnet doesn't seem as much fun to play as Polly or Maisie. Of course, I play the older character, which you have to be a *really* good actress to do well, so that's why I think he cast me in the part. But still, I am not in as many dance or song numbers as they are. I could have played any of those other parts well too.

Tomorrow is Gwen's birthday. We're going out to the Outback Steak House to celebrate with some other friends. I hope I make it—I am so exhausted just thinking about it! So much to do . . . no time to do it!

Teresa

Mar 4
Dear Diary,

This week in school they made time for this special presentation. They do that sometimes. Okay, they had this guest visitor this guy Jeremy Hoetzel who got AIDS from a blood transfusion like a really long time ago when he was just a kid. Now I have never been up close and personal with someone with AIDS and this guy was so *HOT*! He had the best attitude about everything too. I don't think I could be that optimistic if someone said I had AIDS. I guess I'd have to be though if I wanted to live.

Anyway, Jeremy's mom was there too talking and she showed us slides of the diseases you can get from having AIDS and whatnot. Then they showed slides of Jeremy with all these famous people. During that part, I could tell he was crying a little bit. He then got up and said that he would take back meeting the president and all those famous people just not to have AIDS anymore. I felt so terrible for him.

Me and my friends were talking afterward about how we would feel if we found out that our boyfriend had AIDS. I said it would be hard but that I would *definitely* continue to be w/that person but obviously not doing anything more intimate than a kiss. My friends said they wouldn't even kiss. Yeah, maybe you reallly can get AIDS from saliva but only if you drink like a gallon of it. Like that is not going to happen—unless you are having one power make-out session! j/k

Jeremy said that he had a girlfriend for like 11 months and I was wondering how she must have felt and why they weren't together anymore. I'm sure she probably broke up w/him because she realized that no matter what, she was going to be hurt, so she did it sooner rather than later. I wonder what it would be like if you knew you could be w/a person who you could spend 6 months with and be absolutely and totally happy KNOWING that after those 6 months that they would die, could I handle that? Who would do that?

Emma

3/4, 5 p.m.

Today first period me & MB were bored as usual. We didn't want to pay attention and MB had to tell me something so we just wrote back & forth. We always do and we never get caught, not once.

EM—So TJ called me like out of the blue. We haven't really talked in a few days. Well, when he called he was like when do you get ur license & I was like 48 days and he was like oh that's kinda long to wait. Then he said once u get ur license we should hang out a lot so I said I guess so. He kept saying no I want to do that and it was kinda weird. I didn't expect him to be saying that. Where were u last nite? w/b

Look, that's good that he wants to hang out w/you though right? He is def. a little weird . . . but that would be cute w/you two, right? Are you going to hang out with him then over the weekend? Stupid Cliff has to work Friday and Saturday again. This really stinks a lot. I may pick him up after work on Sat. to go do something, but I am not really sure if that'll happen. Yesterday I had SAT class until like 9. I'm not sure if I can go and get my nails done today. I have to ask my mom plus I have to see how much work I have tonight. There's a prom meeting after school. Are you going to that or to the Community Club meeting? w/b

Did I tell you I was going snowboarding on Friday? So today after school I'm going to rent boards for all of us. So I doubt I can go w/you. Sorry. Look, maybe we can go 2morrow nite or another time? Like Saturday during the day do u wanna hang out? Actually I might have to work Sat. too but if I get home early wanna do something? Have u talked to Sherelle lately? I haven't. Really I don't even bother n e more b/c she always says she'll call back and you know how it is.

I can't go tomorrow because I have a

tutor and I have to babysit of course. I don't want to but I need the money. I totally forgot you were going snowboarding on Friday. Who are you going with and what time are you going? As far as Saturday, I can definitely go you just let me know. I don't talk to Sherelle a lot either except when I see her at SAT class. All she ever does is talk about Bobby, right?

On Friday, I won't be in school like I said b/c we're playing hooky but I will be back at nite. Who's going is me, Kevin, Cristina, and Jake. It should be fun.

Jake

March 5

I don't feel much like writing anymore. I just feel kind of pissed off at everyone.

Usually I want to do the right thing, like crack a joke or make everyone feel ok but right now I don't give a shit about anyone else. Even snowboarding kind of sucked.

Kevin

I still keep thinking about that show I saw the other day, the mad show that mentioned Becker md or whatever that disease is that Jake's dad has. If I had one wish and only one it would soooo never be for me & selfish desires no it would be in a heartbeat the wish for all pain and suffering to end. I remember last year in class some teacher asked us if we had something in us that could potentially save like the whole world, would we sacrifice ourselves to do that? Like if we had some special immunity that could cure the world of some awful disease, would we kill ourselves for that? For me I think doing something like that would give me so much pride of course I would do that. I hope that someday I can go with all the honor and the dignity that I dream of, knowing that I made a difference in at least a few people's lives. I know that probably sounds so stupid but it's true, it's how I feel right now.

Btw today snowboarding totally was great even tho my knees are ruined and we all really were hurting afterward. What a fun afternoon like when Marybeth wiped out and we were all laughing pretty hard. Too bad that school completely blows and I am feeling all serious & shit. Oh God, I am so sore like I can't feel my knees or my ass. Ta ta

marybeth

March 6th

I can't believe how much I ache fm. yesterday. Ouch! Here is my pass from snowboarding with Kevin & Jake & Cristina:

```
MOUNT ALTA VISTA


LOWER MTN
Adult
MAR 05
$25.00
Nontransferable
```

My sis Kyra called me tonite & we were talking about her getting married, which is so cool. We have not been talking 4 like a long time & suddenly she is like calling me. It's weird but I like it.

Emma

Okay, so I just wanted to say something about my good friend Roger who I actually have not seen that much lately, but the two of us are really really close. For the past two weeks he has been the biggest jerk even though *HE* was the one who wanted to take me to the semi when I thought Cliff couldn't go. Well, we have not talked because he wouldn't talk to me ok and he was acting all weird on me. And then after the first week of him not talking to me, well, I just stopped trying to talk to him. I thought he didn't care. And I was so mad that he didn't care because good friends are supposed to care about each other. I hate fighting with him.

But then last night he IMed me and I almost fell over. I didn't even think that he had AOL because he is never on. I knew that I didn't do anything wrong. *SO* when he IMed me and said *HE* was sorry I was sooooo glad. He blamed it on being in a bad mood for weeks, which he was. I was not the only person he wasn't talking to. Ever since the last hockey play-off he has been in a really bad mood and I was not the only one who noticed it. But once he said, "I'm sorry," it like made everything better. Yesterday in school he jumped me and gave me a huge hug and it felt so good to hug him again. It was like the way it used to be. He said he would take me to the prom if Cliff couldn't go.

Feeling Loved Feeling Loved

<u>Teresa:</u>
Oh, boy! Who doesn't want to be loved? Who doesn't yearn for someone to care for them? Everyone does! It's a fact! I think about it every day—how a person could love me and not intentionally hurt me. It sounds too good to be true, but it is true. I just hope it happens to me! Feeling loved ties in with fitting in, having people who care about you and accept you. I haven't been in love yet, but we'll see!!!!!

<u>Kevin:</u>
I feel A lot beTTeR About myself. If I weReN't loved I would be upseT And not hAppy but oh well, I just deAl wiTh whAt I geT And if love coMes ARound then it's cool.

<u>Katie:</u>
There is no better feeling in the entire world than knowing someone loves you. I have wonderful parents, sister, brother as

well as Grandpa and a million uncles, aunts, and cousins. I have wonderful friends who care about everything I do. Not to forget Brad. I get warm and fuzzy just talking about him.

Jake:

Once Jonny said he loved me as a bestest best friend and Kevin too and that felt good to know someone was there.

Marybeth:

It's important to know that someone looks 4ward to seeing you or talking to you. Even if it's not a gf or bf b/c family is just as important 2 me, supporting me. . . .

Billy:

I remember the feeling of being loved by Blair D. and that was just way too much then. But now I look back and I can see how much I threw away. I took her for granted because she

Feeling Loved Feeling Loved

was just a freshman then and I was into myself
too much to realize what I had. She was great
and she would have done anything for me.

Emma:
    Being loved by a boyfriend is a
totally different kind of love than
parent love. Katie and I talk about this
all the time because she feels about
Brad like I feel about Cliff.

Baxter:
    My family loves me unconditionally no matter what
I do or say. Of course, that kind of being loved isn't
quite the same thing as it would be with Megan or
Jessica. But then again being loved doesn't have to be a
big deal. Sometimes it can just be.

Teresa

Dear Diary,

Here's my horoscope from the book that tries to tell me everything about my life but always lies:

L O V E

Libras have an instinct for beauty and love, coupled with an innate ability to "charm the pants off" anybody! You truly enjoy lavishing attention on your love and will do whatever necessary to make them happy. In fact, what you really want is to be the best mate they've ever had . . . or dreamt of having. But it's not unusual for a Libra to feel alone in a relationship, not knowing how to reach out and ask for love in return for what you are so willing to give. Libras thrive in committed relationships, especially with someone solid and confident who helps you to make your many dreams (and you have a lot of them) come true.

I know I am always complaining because I don't have someone to love or someone to love me in my life, but I can't help it. Love is just all around me, see? Plus I was just sitting here thinking about how much I love my work. Like today for example is Sunday and I miss those little kids soooo much. I feel like I constantly need to be with them. It scares me to think how lonely I will be in September when I have to quit them for field hockey. That upsets me soooo much! Right now I cannot even go 1 single weekend without them, let alone 3 months!!! It makes me so happy to know that in some way I make those kids happy. This past Valentine's Day we all sent each other cute valentines too and that was awesome. I need to know that in 10 years they can look back and remember me and I will *NEVER* forget working with them.

Marybeth

March 7th

Yesterday I had to work at 7 a.m.—*YUCK*! I was only supposed to work until 11 but I switched shifts w/this other girl and then I had to stay at work until 12. Afta all that, all I could do was come home & take a huge nap. Last nite I went over to Matt's. It wuz me, him, and this kid Lance. At like 8:30 we went to the movies. It was really funny, this movie called *Office Space*. Today I met up w/Emma & she went to get her nails done. They look real cute. Now I have to go work again from 2:15 to like 7:15 so I dunno what I'll do later. Since it's Sunday maybe I will just hang at home.

Baxter

March 8

This weekend was ok. Friday night, Derek and I went to see *Cruel Intentions*. It was so *GOOD*. Even though driving with him in my car was like driving with my mother for some reason. Then he and I went to Taco Bell.

Saturday I had to pick Derek up from the station. He went shopping or whatever and needed a ride home late. Then at night I went over to Megan's place just for no reason. Well, I found out something so bad. She's seeing Russ! He's another guy in our class. Actually, he's in the play with Katie right now. He's one of the leads. Oh no, that *SUCKS*!!!!

Another horrible thing is that I am bombing chem.

Okay, one good thing is my car got fixed. Lights!

Katie

March 8
@ 5:20 P.M.

Here's the basic rundown of what I did on Saturday:

8:30–11 SAT tutor. And I broke 1300 on a test!
11–12   Nap
12–1   Shower; get ready to go

1–5:30   Dance rehearsal for *BF*
5:45–7   Go & get costume for play

There was this thrift shop in the next town and we were all having a *really* hard time finding a costume for me. Everyone had on these cute outfits, but there wasn't anything that looked a little older. I didn't want bloomers with some other weird thing going on. That's what they're wearing most of the time in the show—that and flapper dresses, which is closer to what I had to purchase.

Oh, another Saturday thing was that it was Brad and my 6-month anniversary! We went to see a romantic movie, *Message in a Bottle*. It was a lot of fun. Brad is just one of the few people in the whole world who has the ability to make me totally relax. My life has been crazier than ever these past 2 weeks but when I am in his arms, I forget everything. On Saturday for our anniversary, Brad bought me pink roses and this toy sailboat! The story is that yesterday we went searching all day for the perfect sailboat for the play but Brad is the one who found it! He's the best. And today begins yet another hellish week but I am so filled with anticipation, nervousness, and excitement!

Kevin

Ok Saturday was pretty cool me, Jake, and Lazlo went with Rosie to this party at one of our friends' houses it was pretty fun. Then afterward Rosie & I got a little freaky deaky and that was *VERY* cool. Um, so as usual I did nothing at all the next day LOL I was tired and bored b/c Sundays are really the only day of the week when I can sleep late b/c of working on Sat. morn. So I go ahead Sunday & sleep in. Oh yeah, I had this major chem test on ions yesterday. Shoulda studied more for that one.

Jake

March 9

There was this kickin party this weekend and Kevin was totally hooking up w/Rosie Wellner. When he hooks up I am usually proud of him. I would want that for myself.

At this party I was alone with no woman. I just got drunk and was the life of the party. Just cracking jokes and playing around since I have to do something when I don't have the ladies to play with.

School is pretty bad these days. I have to start studying more but I have so much work. I guess I will figure it all out later. I need the cash for now. I am getting at least 3 or 4 leads every time I go in.

Teresa

Dear Diary,

I just got back from the photo store, where I got my pictures from the trip to see Jaclyn at college! I didn't take that many because I didn't bring my camera with me when we went to that frat party but that's okay.

We look pretty good the night we went to the party. That was so fun! I am so psyched about what we did. I have this one photo of Will and Dean and they look like such hotties. But unfortunately the truth of the matter is that they lied to us. They said they were half brothers and we believed them! But the truth is they were lying the whole time and it was all a bunch of crap. So now I hate them both.

Wendy is upset about the whole trip though on account of her bf. She doesn't ever want to go back there because of what she did. I don't blame her. He would be really upset of course if he knew what happened.

Emma

3/9, 7:45 p.m.

Yesterday I decided to go driving around with Marybeth to look at the place where Cliff's ex-girlfriend Rebecca lives. The two of us looked her up in the phone book. She lives in the next town over, which is really really small. They don't even have a school. Anyway, we made this one turn right onto the street where Rebecca happens to live. Oh well, so we drove around the block and saw it. Cliff of course has no idea that we did any of this and if he did know I think he would kill me. He would seriously go crazy. He would be really really mad at me and I dunno so I won't tell him. Or maybe I'll just tell him another time like a long time from now.

Things with me and Cliff are going really good. He's coming over to watch *Dawson's Creek* this week. He came over to watch it last week too. People think that is really cute. Plus I am glad he is coming over because I haven't seen him a lot. Not since Saturday and that's a long time for us. I mean, I talk to him all the time, but that's not the same thing. I wanna see him.

I have this great photo of me and him that someone took at the semi and his eyes are closed, but he still looks ok. The only thing is that he's wearing this stupid necklace in the picture. I hate that stupid necklace so much. It is gold and big and says FUBU or something. I told him not to wear it but he didn't listen. I think the letters on it must stand for something but I dunno what. I guess I am mostly used to it by now. My mom didn't have to see it, thank God. He was nice enough to take it off for the pictures at my house, so that was good. I didn't want that stupid thing in *my* pictures!

I ♥ Cliff soooooooo much!

Billy

3-10

This week was the same ol' plus a little more stuff that I had to do, I guess not quite as monotonous as usual. The play rehearsal every day really cuts into your life, and I feel like I am just going bet. the play & sports. Over last wkend I was there in the auditorium the whole time and I prob. should have been checking out lacrosse. But then 2 days ago, March 8, I skipped the 3 to 5 part of the play practice and I went to get my physical & the required forms to play lacrosse. Does any of it make sense going back and forth? Anyway, it's mad drama trying to make everyone happy. Like if I didn't get my physical ok sheet to the coach so I could practice then I would be kicked off or whatever. That would be no good. I need 6 practices total to end up playing in the scrimmage. I wonder if I will be able to do it. But then of course on the other hand I have to go to as many play rehearsals as I can too so I won't get kicked out of the show. Mad drama, like I said.

Marybeth

March 10th
My math teacher has the *FATTEST* arms oh my God I swear & it can be such a boring class sometimes but oh well! Jeez, my school days are not what I'd call exciting are they? I did just get a pretty decent 2nd period report card though.

Jake

March 10
I think I am doing pretty good this year, considering. We got our report cards in the mail. My parents were really proud of me. I got a D in chemistry last marking period but I brought it up to an A– this period. So that's like a B– average or more so far. Midterms and finals were hard, but not so bad. I really don't care anymore about tests. I just do what I can do. There's too much going on.

Kevin

3/10

It's Wednesday and I got that freakin chem test back the one I thought I did ok on well I was *WRONG* b/c I got a freakin D on it and I am now *seriously* doin bad in that class and it pisses me off b/c I am studying too. I am doing decent in math but it's kinda hard we're doing logarithms now & it is hard freakin stuff. In English the teacher I am ready to kill her what a bitch she is constantly singling me out for some reason and yelling and screaming at ME and just me. I hate her & I am at the point where I yell back at her and make fun of her to her face now it's sooooo bad. I swear that auto shop is my only savior in the entire day it is the absolutely only class that doesn't completely bore me to shit. I love it.

Ok so recently the days have been goin a little faster, which is good def. a good thing. Lacrosse has started. I'm not playing though. I wanna b/c Jake does and so does Billy but then again I will never letter in the sport, so what's the point. It'll be all that hard work for nothing. I will miss the team thing and all that fun but I would rather work and make more & more money for stuff this spring. So I just won't play.

As far as Rosie goes, me and her are getting along ok but it's like I just don't know what to do now. I do like her but I know we won't go out like for real for a while now. I want her really really bad but then I

105

don't know. Sometimes I think we wouldn't make that good a couple. Or then I think maybe I don't wanna be in a real committed relationship right now. I am happy with friendship. I know if we got a little closer I would be happy since we have a lot to kid about we're not ever bored or anything. Um the other thing is that I think about wanting other people besides Rosie. I think about them all the time. It's no big surprise, just Cristina a little bit and of course Renee that girl from lifeguarding b/c she is slammin. That's about it ta ta I'm out.

Emma

3/10, 5:22 p.m. exactly

Things with Cliff are good but I have mostly been so busy with school, it's unbelievable. Plus for the past 2 days I have felt really sick and I have been going to SAT class 3 times a week. I can't wait until that is over. I have to take the SATs in exactly one week, well, in 10 days, a weekend away. I'm not looking forward to them at all. I just have to concentrate and use whatever Princeton Review has taught me. They really have helped so I should be fine taking the test. The only thing is that we all have to go take them at Grimes! I can't believe it since it's like our biggest school competitor. I hate that building too. And it is pretty far away from here too. My dad will have to take me and then wait around for like 3 hours since that's about how long the test is. I dunno I am just hoping they are not as hard as I am afraid they will be. Some people say they are easy but I dunno because those people are like the supersmart ones.

Yesterday I got a progress report from chemistry. My stupid teacher sent me one because I got a failing grade on the last test. It's not like I was the only one who failed. I told my mom beforehand so she knew. She told me I had to focus more so I told her that I would focus. And when the actual progress report came in the mail yesterday she really wasn't that mad. Well, when she happened to open the envelope I was on the computer and the telephone and she got upset saying that I had to get off right now and talk to her. I was on the phone w/Marybeth, who was like what the hell is going on with your mom? Luckily Mom calmed down the minute I hung up. She usually doesn't yell like that so I figured she must have had a bad day at work or something.

Something I got w/Chinese new year symbols. Since I'm born in 1982 I'm a DOG. Cliff is a Rooster.

Pig
1911, 1923, 1935, 1947, 1959, 1971, 1983, 1995, 2007
Superchivalrous, you have great inner strength and spirit. You make few but lasting friendships.

Choose the hare, ram, or horse and avoid the monkey.

Dog
1910, 1922, 1934, 1946, 1958, 1970, 1982, 1994, 2006

Loyal and honest, you are generous and work well with others, though you are sometimes too critical. You are well suited to the hare and the tiger and ill suited to the dragon and the ram.

Rooster
1909, 1921, 1933, 1945, 1957, 1969, 1981, 1993, 2005

You are directed to work and seek knowledge, a pioneer who tends to be selfish and lonely. Choose the ox or serpent, but never the hare.

Katie

March 11
@ 5:35 P.M.

Dress rehearsal day! I am so drained, it isn't even funny. Rehearsals every day have been from 3 to 5 and 6 to 10 and I have had voice coaching too every day from 5 to 6 (except today of course). I am so tired!!!

The play is really going beautifully, though; I am so happy about that. This is an ad for it that the school put into the local paper:

The John F. Kennedy Drama Department
and Music Department Present

The Boy Friend

A Musical by Sandy Wilson

Friday and Saturday, March 12–13

8:00 P.M.

JFK East Auditorium

Set on the French Riviera in the 1920s, this fun musical has love, laughs, and some swell dance numbers! Kick up your heels and come!

**Tickets are available from drama club members
and at the door.
Admission: Students $2.50 and adults $5.00**

For further information, contact JFK High School at 555-9028.

Mine and Deke's act is so great when we sing "You Don't-Want-to-Play-with-Me-Blues"; he is so cute! He is this big football player guy, and teaching the two of us to dance together has not been easy or fun! But things are really pulling together and the play should be awesome.

Everyone in the cast has bonded tremendously over the past few weeks. It's the most diverse group of kids, and I have come to a really important realization over the course of the play—being popular isn't important to me in this phase of my life. Actually, let me rephrase that: I want to be well liked and affable; however, hanging out with the wrong groups like the "fast" crowd isn't how I am going to get there. The kids in the arts are the nicest in the school. Everyone is accepted and can feel comfortable in the group from jock to clown to nerd. It may not be the coolest crowd, I know that, but I have met a lot of people and these are undoubtedly the nicest.

Billy

3-11

It's Thursday nite about 12:00 a.m. and I just got done with dress rehearsal for *The Boy Friend* and it all looks pretty good except I missed my cue once and I got kicked around a little on the stage. Katie looks good too esp. when she and Deke have this one dance number it is a real laugh riot.

I am actually glad in some ways that the play is almost ending because I need to buckle down and deal w/SATs. I did some prep course so that should help me get my scores into the 1300s I hope. That is my goal for March 20.

Baxter

March 11

Great news! No chem. test today. I got myself all nervous for nothing. Plus I'm taking a psychology elective that's very interesting. We have inside jokes in class and sometimes we can be childish but it's fun. The most important thing is to laugh. When I was a little kid I always wondered what it would feel like to get older. I guess this is it. This is definitely it.

My Happiest Childhood Moment

Teresa:

I have soo many! First I would have to say just all the times going to my grandma and grandpa's house for Easter or Thanksgiving and being with my whole family was always fun. Then I would have to say meeting all of my friends and my BFF Wendy in Kindergarten and then meeting Gina in 4th grade when she chose me to be her best friend . . . I was honored. And I remember this time when I was in 5th grade and a boy that was in 7th grade asked for my number and wanted to dance with me! Anyway, I had an awesome childhood that I miss very much but am happy to have experienced.

Billy:

To be dead honest, I can't think of a really happy memory. I think I remember one good birthday party maybe, but otherwise there hasn't really been an extravagant moment, no utopia here. My life has some bad memories unfortunately.

My Happiest Childhood Moment

Emma:

   I wanna get close to my cousin Ed
again. When we were little we were soooo
close. I used to always go to his house
and sleep in his room because he had like
2 beds in his room and we would always
stay up too late talking. It makes me
happy just to think about it now.

Kevin:

   I dunno if this is my happiest
memory or not but it is A good one.
It was from Easter morning when
we lived in our old house on the
other side of town. I had this
infatuation with the Pillsbury
Doughboy for some reason And so I
would walk Around poking everyone in
their tummies going, "Whooooo!" It
was so funny. I remember this one
morning I woke up to this Easter
basket And in it was A Pillsbury
Doughboy doll. I sat Around for
hours just poking it in the tummy.
Nothing bothered me.

My Happiest Childhood Moment

Katie:
On my dad's side of the family I have like 24 cousins, some ridiculous number, and when I was a little girl, my aunt would have these huge family reunions and weekend escapes to her house on the coast. It was like a mansion, her house. And I remember everything about that place — pumpkin carving in the fall, bonfires on the beach, my uncle's weird recipe for bread pudding with apricots, which we always fed to the dog under the table, lying in the hammock, and so many more.

Baxter:
Once my parents surprised me and my brother Jerry with a trip to Disney World. They just woke us up at like 4 a.m. and said we're going to Disney World. We didn't believe them until they showed us the bags were all packed. Someday I will do that kind of stuff with my own kids.

Marybeth:
Best childhood memory = riding my bike

My Happiest Childhood Moment

for hours around the block & passing the
same thing over & over but I was in my
own little world so I didn't care.

Jake:

Way before my dad got sick, we
used to fish and crab together in the
bay. He took me there when I was little.
I have this picture of him smiling with
my little sister in one arm since she
couldn't stand up yet and I'm there
holding his hand. I don't remember the
last time I have seen him smile like
that. I crack jokes now and he still
doesn't smile as big as that.

Emma and **Marybeth**

March 12th

Yesterday my sister was telling me that Sherelle has been beeping this kid Andy from Webster and has been trying to start all this shit with him. She is the biggest instigator. What about Bobby, right? I said yeah that she probably would do something like that because that is just how she is being lately. I do miss those Webster guys though. Hey, did TJ ever call you back? Duh, so many people asked me for my chemistry and I made so many excuses. It's funny. w/b

No one has asked me for my chem! Well, TJ did, but he didn't want the extra credit. It was something else what Sherelle did. Why does she do stupid shit like that? Anyway, yeah, TJ called me last nite but I wuz sleeping. Oh well. I did talk to my friend Teddy from work and he keeps asking me to hang out. He said I should ask u 2. I was like I'll see what's up. He was like look, when you come we don't have to do anything illegal. I was like ok how nice. What was that? w/b

I think we should go hang out with the guys from webster. It would really piss off Sherelle but we should do it anyway. Who the hell knows why she does what she does, she's just <u>LAME</u>. So, Teddy from your job wants to hang out? He is so funny. Does he still have a thing for you? How funny that he said that we wouldn't do something illegal. Where does he live? If we ever do hang with him we better not tell Cliff because he'll get mad. I feel so much better today than I did earlier this week. The next time Andy calls, let's make plans to hang out or something. w/b

I can't hang out this weekend b/c I've got to work both nights. Yeah, Teddy wanted me to come over after school but I said there was no way I was walking all that way to his place. I told him I might have track but he said so what come anyway. Anyway, this class really sux, doesn't it? w/b

If you really want I can drive you to Teddy's house. He lives over by the Quik Check, right? Of course that's only if you want to go. Are you going to track today? I will take you home from school if you want. Let me know later if you need a ride. BTW are you going to the play tonight? I want to go and see Katie.

I have to babysit. Maybe I'll go on Sat. instead. Maybe I should ask Teddy to go w/me HA HA HA j/k.

Katie

March 12
@ 3:50 P.M.

Show day! I am so nervous. Brad picked me up from school yesterday and today and I came right home so I could focus! Brad is such a godsend, I swear! He's been so supportive throughout this whole ordeal of the show and all. I was diagnosed with strep throat on Tuesday and thankfully my medicine has knocked it out of my system—I think! I am seriously going to die from the size of the butterflies in my stomach right now. So many people are coming out to support me in the play, like over 60 between the 2 nights, and it is flattering but nerve-racking. I am really excited and scared all at the same time.

@ 12:30 A.M. the next morning—yeah!

WOW! I am tired, happy, excited, and about a million other feelings all mixed into one! Opening night was a tremendous success! Everyone did great and I am so proud. Deke and I have the curtain call right before the end and people were yelling and screaming. I got eight bunches of flowers tonight. I felt so honored that so many people care so much about me. Emma was so sweet—she did my hair! And my cousin came and brought me this huge bunch of flowers *before* the show even happened. The whole preparation process began at 4:30 when my hair was pulled up and curled and I was costumed. Emma stayed with me the whole time, which I really appreciated. Sherelle came tonight with Bobby, and Gwen came too with her boyfriend. Marybeth didn't come. I wonder what she did instead.

The best feeling in the world is the sense of accomplishment you get from doing a play. Tonight was amazing. From the moment when Deke and I walked onstage for the curtain call until the moment I arrived home was just so great. So much love and support were all around me. The cast totally felt like a family in so many ways. We went to this local restaurant afterward—it was the entire cast plus Brad and Emma and various other people's boyfriends, girlfriends, etc. We stayed until around 12 or so. I was really tired and didn't feel so good maybe because I have to get up at 6 A.M. to go to this Community Club convention. Otherwise I would have stayed out later.

Brad was so good to come tonight. He came all by himself and he brought me a dozen long-stemmed roses and sat with Emma. He's coming again tomorrow night too. How sweet of him!

Teresa

Mar 12

Dear Diary,

Tonight I was just getting ready to go out to see the school play and my mom walked into my room and started crying. She said, "Vin didn't make the flight." Oh my God, I thought that my brother Vincent's plane had crashed or something and I got so so upset. Vincent was with his friends in the Bahamas for his spring break and something happened to their flight. So he's stranded there and my mom was freaking out all over the place. And then I got so scared by what she was saying that I almost started to cry. But then when she continued and told me how they were stranded on the island because of weather or something, I got mad that she made me think something was really wrong! I didn't understand why she was crying so much. Maybe she was just depressed about her birthday. I don't know.

So tonite Gina and I went to JFK to see the musical, *The Boy Friend*. It was pretty good. I thought that Katie and Billy and everyone did a pretty good job. After last year, I had no hope that the drama dept. could pull off another big show but they did. It was just that last year's graduating class had all the best actors and actresses. In other words, no one expected this production could be good. But it really was! I enjoyed it.

Kevin

3/13

Ok I liked Thursday ok it wasn't that bad I had life guarding as usual but it's all good in the 'hood. I didn't have anything too good happen during the day really and then Fri. went by so quick. That night I had to work from 5:30 to 7:30 and I didn't get home until after 8 and then I was supposed to go to Pizza Hut w/a bunch of people. And I did not feel like going to the play. But then by the time I got to Pizza Hut everyone was leaving and then Jonny got a ticket for seat belts and he was speeding way too much. Oh well. Then today I worked from like 8:15 to 12:30, which wasn't too bad, and I washed my car. Then I went over to Jake's place and we played Bond it's been a pretty lazy wkend.

Billy

3-13

Well, the play this past weekend was great. . . . What a rush. . . . We performed. Katie did well, Deke was great, I did well, we *all* did well. It was a success overall. I even got a bio in the program:

William (Billy) Shim—<u>Bobby</u> <u>van</u> <u>Husen</u>

Billy is grateful to have been chosen to play the role of Bobby in this great musical. A junior at JFK, Billy has been singing all his life and loves it. He is also on both the varsity football and lacrosse teams when he's not onstage. Thanks, Mom and Dad.

The one thing that really got me was at the cast party tonite. It brought a sense of closure on my high school career. The next play I am in will be senior year. And that is scary because at this time of year next year I'll be a senior and then a college freshman and it's scary. It's very scary.

Katie

I am so tired. This morning my mom didn't have the heart to wake me. I only rolled out of bed at noon. Then Rachel Ross and I had to run play errands. We picked up flowers for the director and thank-you cards and whatnot. The two of us are getting along well! It's really nice.

When Rachel and I got home from being out, we helped my mom set up for the cast party. She made such a big deal about everything—how cute! I knew we were in trouble when the caterer brought in 6 trays of hot food and subs that were bigger than the dining room table. We had the party at our house and about 50 or 60 people were here. My friend Jaclyn came from college just to see me too! I was so happy she was there. It is now 2 A.M. I'm waiting for Brad to call.

I just can't get over how great tonight was. We got a packed standing ovation!!! I felt so satisfied. I am so glad I had the opportunity to pursue acting here. If I were at another school, I would not have been good enough probably to even get a medium-sized part. My family came from all over to see the show. Even Brad's parents came. They met my parents for the first time. Luckily everyone has really amiable personalities so they took well to each other. Thank goodness! I will treasure this entire experience forever and ever.

Baxter

March 14

Well, I went to Katie's play last night. It was good. But tonight I feel sick. I just took some NyQuil. I know I am getting a cold. I also went this weekend to another play in the next town with my cousin. That was better. They did *Pajama Game*. It has good music.

I am starting to get very very nervous about the SAT. I have been studying as much as I can all weekend. It has been snowing a lot. Maybe no school tomorrow?

I can't wait for St. Patrick's Day this week.

Katie

March 14
@ 4 P.M.

While most of the other cast members from *The Boy Friend* were probably sleeping in today, I had to arise at 10 for my SAT tutor. She was here until noon. Then I took a simulated SAT to prepare for next week and I scored 1400! That was my target score exactly. I felt so satisfied that my countless hours of SAT work have paid off. Hopefully I will take another full test at home and score higher. God knows I have been working for it. In the past three months I have memorized 400 new vocabulary words, practiced by taking 13 tests, had extensive tutoring, and taken the Princeton Review course. If this doesn't pay off, I don't know what will! I have everything else I need to get into Stanford, I know it. I just need those scores!

Jake

March 14

SATs are a pain in my ass. First of all they are way too long. Then they are also a really unfair judge of how smart you are. I mean anyone can pay a lot of money to learn all these stupid tricks. You go to these places and they tell you how many As and Cs to pick and all these shortcuts to answer questions. They don't even have anything to do with the questions! I have done a little bit of reading and vocabulary studying to try but that's all.

The problem is that right now sure I want to do well but I also don't care. Every test this year basically I don't give a shit about. I am just sick of school and any kind of work. I don't care what college I get into. Well, I do. But just not right now. I am not going to spend my whole time obsessing about that. I want to have fun too. And I want to see my dad more.

Emma

I have to stop worrying so much about the SATs. I have my last prep class this week and the tests are next Saturday. I can't believe it already.

Last night I went with Cliff to see *Cruel Intentions*. It was a really good movie. At first it was a little bit slow, but then it got so much better. It was very exciting because it was like our first date out where we were really *alone*. I told him how happy I was to be out with him alone and he was glad too. He makes me so happy, even when he makes me mad there is a part of me that is happy.

A really weird thing happened tonite my sister Lynn was online and she started talking to Cliff. She was like, Do you really like my sister or what? Cliff was like, Yeah, I do a lot. Then she pushed it and said, Well, do you love her? And Cliff at first didn't answer but then he was like, Yeah, I think that I do. My sister was like, Yeah, but you are young are you *sure* you love her? And Cliff said, Yeah, we are young but who's to say when you know you love someone. Something like that and then he said again that yeah, he did love me. That's what my sister told me he said anyway. I was so happy. I could not believe that he would say all of that to Lynn! Now I know that he really does like me and I don't have to worry anymore.

126

The only thing that bothers me is that he really doesn't like to go out with my friends. Like last nite after we went to the movies, we were supposed to go over to Katie's for her cast party. She asked us both to stop by. But when I asked Cliff about it he made a big deal saying that he wouldn't know anyone and I would just go there and ditch him. I know he thinks that and I know he hates that and I really want him to come with me. So on the way from the movies he kept saying he would not go to Katie's. I was getting pissed. I mean, Katie and even her mom were looking forward to seeing him. He said he did the whole party thing at the Carsons' once—before and after the semi—and he hated it.

Anyway, I ended up just going to the cast party alone. And everyone could tell just by the look on my face that something was obviously wrong and different. Brad and Katie both were asking me where is Cliff, and all I could do is just shrug. I just said don't ask. They didn't say any more.

I ❤ Cliff!

Billy

3-14

Thank God the whole thing with my shoulder is mostly gone. This whole winter the whole arm thing was such a mess. I was planning to get stronger quicker and for lacrosse season but the arm has stopped me from doing anything like physical activity for so long! It has been horrible. I mean, I am so sick of writing with my left hand instead of my right. It was kinda hard to get used to but I have cuz school won't stop just for me! Although I do think some teachers gave me less work.

But hopefully all that is behind me a long time ago. Today was the first scrimmage in lacrosse and I am *so ready* to play! Unfortunately it started snowing really hard and we got destroyed and that's that. I think there is only one thing left to calm my mind and that is *RAW*! No joke I swear I can watch those guys slam each other and I feel better. For whatever reason the violence on that show is actually *funny*.

ViolenceViolence

Baxter:

Teen violence is pretty scary. I mean, it keeps getting worse and worse. I totally blame the parents. I think that it's time for parents to stop being self-centered and start watching their kids. I mean, in Colorado the guns were all over the kids' rooms, and the parents say they didn't know, well, they are full of shit. My mom is always in my room, she cleans it so she knows everything. I also feel that parents need to start staying home with their kids. They shouldn't just ship them off to day care and forget about them.

Katie:

Honestly, I think violence highlighted in the media is the source of all teen problems. My feeling is that if school violence was not so elevated in the news and the media focused on teens helping instead of killing, teenagers would follow the example.

Jake:

Violence is a stupid waste. Something should be done to stop it.

Violence Violence

Teresa:

Violence has become a growing problem in society. It scares me to think of what our world is coming to. Teenage boys and girls from all around the globe are learning how to make bombs and aiming them at schools, a place everyone just assumes is always safe. Moreover, schools shouldn't be looked down upon—they are a place to learn at . . . not a place worthy of destruction. It seems more and more that violence just keeps getting worse and worse. Not only do I think it is a growing problem, but it also can and may affect my personal life sometime in the near future. For this reason, I carry around a can of pepper spray on my key chain. Sure, people laugh at me and think it's a joke, but it's only for my protection. And sure, my town is really safe, but ya never know . . . better safe than sorry. I just think it is a disgrace to religion and humanity that the violence is affecting everyone on every level like one out of every 19 seconds

VioIenceVioIence

someone is raped. That is sad.
Something needs to be done . . . and
fast before we all die from nuclear
poison! Just today my history teacher
asked us what we thought we would be
doing if we had lived in the sixties
and seventies during the Vietnam War.
I immediately said that I would be an
antiwar demonstrator. If the leaders of
my country are going to try to tell me
that killing innocent people is ok, I
will fight them! We say it's our "moral
duty" to stop the communism or what
have you, but we are killing innocent
people and doing it in a vulgar
gruesome way. How moral is that? This
is what I think of when I think of
violence. I hate it so much on all
levels.

Billy:

Come on, violence is everywhere. I feel like it
is such a strong force now and so much a part
of our society that it cannot be stopped. No
matter what legislation the government or the
NRA passes, violence will prevail in this country.

Violence Violence

And the guns, the root of most violence, are
not to blame. The blame is on the teenagers and
other people who murder other individuals over
drugs or women or just because they feel left
out at school. Those are not the victims, they
are the murderers. They should be punished.

Marybeth:

In a few words: There's too much of it.
It is so crazy 2 me what people do. There r
some real sickos out there. But on the other
hand, kids are like cryin out sometimes saying
they're freaked out or po'ed and what—is
anyone paying attention? Why does everyone
ignore the prob. until like 50 people die?
And then y is there like some circus on TV
about it all? Doesn't someone wanna maybe
deal w/the real problem, like IGNORANCE?

Kevin:

That violence that went on in
schools And shit is A crock b/c
obviously the kids who did those bombs
And stuff Are so stupid. They should

Violence Violence

just take out their aggression in the old-fashioned way b/c to bring guns and bombs into school is just retarded. I think everything is def. getting out of control all this violence in our country. People just don't have enough ways to vent or get rid of their anger and they either bottle it up so it explodes at really unfortunate times or they use shit around them like weapons so they make a point. I can't imagine what's happening to this society after all this. How can anyone even want to raise kids in this world seriously?????

Emma:

Violence is a part of life now. It isn't even like bad neighborhoods or places with more crime. There are violent people everywhere—and even more in "safe" places like schools. I get mad too but I just don't understand killing. I think people just want to be noticed maybe. It's definitely a scary time.

133

Kevin

3/15

Hey hey hey Sunday pretty much was me waking up, going over to Jake's for some food and playin Bond all morning & afternoon. It was rather amusing though LOL. So now here I am sitting looking out the window and it is totally snowing out there. The only thing is that when it is real snowy I get fidgety for bed. *BUT* we had off today—yessssss! Snow day!!!! Only thing is that we'll have to make up this day sometime. Some people think we'll do that during the week of Easter and other people say something else. I just say fuck that. Whenever we have a makeup day I plan to just blow it off completely. I am totally cutting. What a stupid thing to do. Tonite the roads were so awful coming home—I couldn't go out again. I had work to do anyhow.

Teresa

Mar 15

Dear Diary,

No school today! It snowed a lot last nite and so today we have no school! I am really happy about it. Now I can catch up with other work and homework that I need to do.

The other day my mom's friend had this psychic over to her house so my mom went over w/a blank tape to record what she said. Before she left, I pleaded w/her to ask the psychic all about me. Ok then she came home w/the tape. The psychic knew right away with like NO information that Mom had 2 kids, a boy & a girl (that's Vincent & me of course), and she knew that I got good grades. She then told my mom that in like 2 weeks a boy would be breaking up with his girlfriend just to go out w/me! She said basically that I would have a boyfriend in 2 weeks!!! Well, 2 weeks from today is this Honors Club meeting and I don't think I am going to meet Mr. Right there and anyway I have not had a boyfriend in like 8 years so now some random strange lady is going to tell me that I am about to get one? I really doubt that a lot. Anyway, I still like Kevin of course but I guess I am *AT LAST* beginning to realize the utter hopelessness of that situation. I mean, I know Kevin likes Rosie a lot, not me. And actually, I am not so sure that she feels the same way for him. Oh well, there is not much I can do.

The thing is I am *majorly* stressing because I have no prom date set up. I know I could always as a last resort ask that kid Jesse from hockey but I totally do not want to because I would not have fun with him! Plus if I come alone, I don't have to pay the extra 10 bucks for him to come too—*YUCK*—what should I do??!

Emma

I have such a headache and my stomach hurts. I have to go to SAT class soon. Today is the last day of the SAT class. I am happy about that. I really hated the class but it did help me out. I can't wait until next Saturday is over. On my last test that I took in class I got an 1150 and that is good for me. I was happy about it. I am also happy about the fact that I am taking the test with my friends. I think I am actually going with Kevin, who said he would drive me. The two of us have gotten along okay lately. It is weird because we never talked before and now we talk all the time in lunch and stuff. It is so funny to me that we actually dated a year ago or so. Seems like so long ago. I really wish we could get close again like we used to be. And Katie says he's being really nice to her too. I wonder why? I wish I could guess what he is thinking.

Kevin

Man oh man the hardest thing about this year is just plain ol' *REALITY*. It hits hard like last year I didn't really think about anything at all I just did whatever and now it's like I have my license and I know I am growing up cause of that. I have to do really good in school esp. this year cause this year is a lot harder and more learning has been required. Then there's all this shit all the time about how we have to get ready for college and all that and independence just feels so big like too much too fast. I don't think I wanna grow up I just wanna sleep and not have to work a lot I like it w/under 20 hours a week like for the rest of my life. I also get worried like how do I pick just one thing to do for the rest of my life. I'll just have to get used to it.

Katie

March 17
@ 8 P.M.

Happy St. Patrick's Day!

Today is always a sad day for me because I have memories stuck in my mind from 3 years ago, which was the last time I saw one of my grandmothers alive (my mom's mom). The next day she went into the hospital and did not come out. She was so much like me; I used to look up to her so much. I still really do.

Let's see, on a happier note I stayed up with my mom last nite and baked about 20 loaves of soda bread for this supper fair our church is having. I took 2 loaves to the guidance office, especially for this one secretary Mrs. Hurley, who is a full-blood Irishwoman. She appreciated it very much I know. The whole office where she sits is decorated with shamrocks during the month of March—she even has shamrock chair cushions that she brings in. I heard she made 65 pounds of corned beef for a teacher buffet at lunch. I couldn't go because I had a trip! Oh well!

We went out today to this music competition, where this group of handpicked kids auditioned for this regional sing-along. It was 100 percent successful. Hopefully our school and county won the competition so we can go represent our area at the state tournament. Hopefully! It would be such a huge honor.

Jake

March 17
Why do they call this day St. Patrick's Day again? Who was this guy? Dad is feeling like crap. So am I.

Emma and **Marybeth**

March 17th

Happy St. Paddy's Day to Y-O-U. Whassup? This class sux again!

Yesterday at SAT class, Sherelle was talking about how we are going to dinner Friday at 8, and she's having this other party on Saturday night but we can go to both nights if we want. I dunno I think I would feel dumb going twice. Are you going to dinner with her tonight for her birthday? Do you think Cliff is going to be mad that I am planning to go to the prom with Roger? He isn't going w/that other girl BTW. I want to tell Cliff about it face-to-face since he doesn't want to go anyhow. I hope he's not mad. Do you think Sherelle will pass her driving test today? w/b

Well yeah of course I think u should tell Cliff face 2 face! Oh no, I won't go to Sher's on Sat. b/c I have to work. I am so bored right now. And yeah I think Sher will pass her test. You know, Em, I think it's ree-lee cute that Roger will be taking you 2 the prom. Ugh my legs hurt right now so much from track. I hate it so much. Oh my God I am tired too. Mick Lazlo picked me up for school today at like 7:45 and I was like what are you doing here so early? I am SO BORED. Nothing left 2 write!!!!!!!

Oh except I actually saw Cliff last nite. He was @ work. OK w/b

I really hope Cliff doesn't get all mad about the Roger thing. But it's not like me and Roger are anything more than friends. Cliff is the one I ♥!!! I am so excited about going with him actually. He will be so nice. My friend Randi is psyched too. We decided to go in the same limo. Plus Roger says everything is paid for. BTW that's cool that you saw Cliff last nite, me too. I had to go buy eggs. Weird about Mick coming in soooo early. Where does he park? Are you going to track again today?? Oh God what is Baxter laughing about???? I am waiting now for a beep from Sherelle. She said she'd beep me as soon as she got her license.

Baxter

March 17

It's a pretty boring day for St. Patrick's Day. Except that Sherelle just called me. She got her license!!!! I am so happy for her. What a cool thing that her birthday is today. I'm sure she's sick of hearing about it. Oh well.

The SATs are only 3 days away. It feels so ominous. I wish I didn't have to take them. I feel nervous physically. That's how it is.

Teresa

Dear Diary,

I called Jesse. I held off as long as I could but I called. I have no idea why exactly. We talked for a little while and it was good but I am *really* going to dread having to ask him to the prom if that is what I have to do. I really do NOT want to do that under any circumstances.

SATs are in 2 days, on Saturday. I have so so so so so so much pressure on me. I want so much to be a Reynold's Scholar, which is someone who scores a certain score on each part of the SATs. And this after all is my future—if I don't do well then how is my life going to be? I realize that I can take them again, but I'd rather not have to do that. I am so hoping to get over 1300 but at this point I am thinking it won't happen.

Kevin

3/18

What is going on here ohhh man I just turned off the TV & *Rocky III* was on man that is like my

141

favorite movie of all time I was so psyched to see it on that I taped it. This week went by really fast. After work on Tuesday, I got a new beeper cause the screen on my other one died cause I dropped it one too many times. Sooo it's a top view one very cool I like it a lot. Now school on the other hand has been pretty shitty and boring this week nothing has changed much but I am dealing w/it I guess. Today I was like falling asleep in classes but then after school me and Manny went to get bracelets for the DMB concert and that was way cool but oh gotta go late for work more later.

Marybeth

March 18th

I finally started track. I have been running so much & my legs are so sore. I don't think I have *ever* felt pain like this before.

Yesterday was Sherelle's b-day and she got her license! We're all supposed to go out w/her either tomorrow or Sat. I dunno which one yet.

So I've been talking a lot to Teddy, that guy from work. We talk all the time. He's a real cutie. I think I like him but I dunno. We seem to connect but we lead 2 totally different lifestyles. I will have to see what happens—if I can wait. Sher says he's cute. I dunno.

Katie

We all went out for Sherelle's birthday tonight and it was fun. SATs are tomorrow and we talked about that a little bit. There was a conflict of interest between those who care about the SATs and those who don't care. Frankly, I don't care anymore what anyone thinks. If I care about a test enough to go home at 10, then what's wrong with that? Marybeth doesn't seem to care, and that's fine for her because I am not about to lecture anyone. I do my thing, she does her thing. All I know is that I have come way too far to throw away a shot at doing well on this test for one stupid night out. I am not nervous either, just anxious to get it over with. But not too anxious. I am certainly prepared.

Billy

3-19

SATs tomorrow! Oh wow it's Fri. nite and this past week all I have been doing is dreading my chem and math tests. All week I have been doing nothing but bulling ahead in those subjects. Well, they're over at last. Okay so chem went well but math went even better cuz . . . it was *MOVED* to Monday actually. Ha ha ha that is the greatest news. Of course next Thurs. I

143

have *another* chem test on chapters 11 and 12. That one will be the real killer. Tonite after lacrosse practice I think I wanna go to the movies. Who cares about the SATs, right? If I don't know it now I never will. Is this what junior year has all been leading up to?

Tests Tests Tests

Marybeth:
   Since tests don't bother me (none do) I never get bugged out or make myself bring along anything but me and whatever will b will b, and the same goes even 4 the SAT.

Billy:
   I'm fixating on where we're taking it. Our school is so dark and that works so against me usually. Like when I get bad grades the room seems to get darker and darker but when I get a nice grade the room is bright. Weird but that is the way it is. I can only hope the SAT room is really bright.

Emma:
   When I have a major test my stomach gets all funny because of nerves, but I have never had any nightmares before. Sometimes me and my friends will quiz each other beforehand, but I like studying alone so I can get more out of it.

Tests Tests Tests

Baxter:
Before most tests I pray to God.

Teresa:
I have decided that most of the time I can study for hours for a test and I still will do poorly. So I won't really stress over tests now except physics. No matter what I study or what I do, there will always be something on a physics test that I do not understand!

Kevin:
Um I hAve this stone-cut BuddhA when you Rub its tummy it bRings you good luck, but sometimes it doesn't woRk too well foR me. Even so I bRing it And hAve since fReshmAn yeAR, like only to exAms though, but I think I will def. keep it in my pocket foR the SAT.

Tests Tests Tests

Katie:
  When I was younger, I'd get so nervous on test or quiz days I couldn't even eat, but I have come to realize that it means so little in the long scheme — with the exception of the SAT. I need all the luck I can get with this one. The SAT is the most important test I will ever take. And that is a LOT of pressure.

Jake:
  I will do what I can to finish the test that's it. I don't believe in luck or rabbit's feet.

Emma

3/20, 8:00 p.m.

Well today was the big day. The SATs were today. It wasn't too bad getting there. I went with a friend and because my mom called for specific directions, it was real easy to find. The tests weren't that bad either. The math one was definitely hard for me because I hate math a lot. The verbal section was easier. We started the test at like 9 and we were done right at 12. At first they seemed long and then time just started to go by very quickly. After the SATs I went with Pam to lunch. She drove me there. I feel so full right now still because I pigged out on a sundae, which came with lunch. Last night I went out with a bunch of people for Sherelle's birthday to celebrate her getting her license. Well there was one bad moment when I told her I would have to leave a little early because of the SATs the next day and she gave me this look. I was so annoyed. I mean she was taking them too but she didn't think that was any reason to leave her party. Whatever. I was so pissed that she had no reason to be mad at me. I mean my mom wanted me to come home and I wasn't going to argue with her about it. The truth is I wasn't the only person who left early so did Mick and Betsy Geffen and Katie too. Finally though after like giving me looks for the whole beginning of the nite, she snapped out of it and was cool to me and everyone else again. It's funny because in the end we all wound up leaving at the same time anyway.

When we left the restaurant we decided to all follow each other home and I was the designated leader so I pulled onto the parkway and then out of nowhere Sherelle comes flying past me. I really wanted her to get pulled over for doing that because last weekend my cousin got pulled over at that same spot and the two of them drive the same car. She eventually slowed down and then was acting like she was so cool or something saying, I really burned you on the parkway. And I was like, my pickup wasn't too fast so I couldn't keep up with her. The truth is I don't really care because she is going to be the one who gets into an accident if she keeps driving like she does.

By the way I still have *NOT* told Cliff about the whole prom date thing with Roger. I am definitely going with Roger. I don't think Cliff will get mad, but who knows. We're supposed to get together later tonight so I will tell him then. I just have to do it in person and not over the phone. We're supposed to go to this girl Deena's in our class she's having a party to celebrate the SATs being over. I hope it's more fun than yesterday.

Baxter

I cannot believe what happened yesterday with that *BITCH* Miss Shapiro. She pulled me out of class. She told me that she was going to just put this other kid Ariella's name on the writing contest because she claims she saw Ariella doing *ALL* the work and not me. *THAT BITCH!!!!!!* I told her that I wrote everything and she said she wasn't too sure about that. I said are you calling me a liar and she said that she wasn't too sure about a lot of things with me and Community Club. I can't believe the nerve of her! I really had to leave that room fast before I told her off. Because the thing is you just can't tell off a teacher no matter how much you want to or no matter how deserved it is. And this was deserved. What a total bitch. No one and I mean *NO ONE* has ever made me so angry all at once. I was shaking she pissed me off so much. How can she do that to me? Why would she do that to me? I wanted to spray paint her car or something. I will *NEVER* again speak to that evil monster as long as I live.

p.s. The SATs were okay.

Katie

Well, the SATs are over. Until June at least because
I will probably take them again then to raise my
scores. Okay, let's start at the beginning. My day
began at 6:30 A.M. when I arose and ate breakfast.
Then Gwen picked me up at 7 A.M. and some other
girls in our little group followed us in their cars to the
muffin shop. I have read somewhere that kids do better on the SATs if they have breakfast with their
friends first. Then we had to go all the way to Grimes
and thank God we had left so early because of course
we got lost. It was funny because we had to pull into
this gas station and we were all these cars following
each other so we were honking and yelling out the
window and we just couldn't get it together. We just
didn't know how to get there! Fortunately I ran a
block and this guy at 7-Eleven knew where we had to
go. He was really nice to us too. We made it *barely* on
time to the school with only minutes to spare.

The actual SATs themselves were a comical experience. It was like something out of an episode of
Seinfeld. I was in this room with Sherelle and
Marybeth actually. First of all, the test is really strict
about IDs and I was first to get into the room. My
seventh-grade passport photo looks so different than
me now so the woman hassled me a little bit, but I
made it in. I compared gaining entrance to that room

151

to like gaining entrance to Ellis Island, or so I imagined. It was so nerve-racking. There were five rejects without IDs in our room alone!

The good thing was that I was prepared. Dad bought me two new backup calculators in addition to my giant monster-sized one that graphs. My mom sharpened an entire box of pencils for me. Of course my friends all tortured me for being so prepared, like Sherelle and Marybeth especially! However, Sher changed her tune when her calculator batteries died before she even took the math test and I lent her one of my extras. Even the proctors made a comment about how prepared I was.

In the middle of the test I had this huge allergy attack, which drove everyone else in the room nuts and made me more than a little bit self-conscious. But I wasn't the worst. This gross boy who was sitting behind Sherelle kept coughing and coughing and finally she turned right around and said, "Would you shut up!" Midway through the test I asked one proctor a question and when she didn't know the answer, she screeched halfway across the room, "Hey, do you lose points for this?" I was mortified. It was soooo embarrassing! But I survived and I hope I did well!!!

After the test I went shopping for prom dresses with Gwen, and later on Brad took me out to dinner to celebrate the fact that the dreaded test was *finally* over!

Jake

The SATs are done. Thank God they are done.
I am so sick of everything.

Kevin

3/20

SATs are done ok first things first I had that awful math test yesterday that was kind of hard. I really thought I was gonna do good but later I found out b/c the teacher graded it in like 2 minutes that I actually got a freakin C on it. The tests in that class are the only things that keep me from getting As and that's that. So after that after school I just chilled for a while and hung w/Jake & this chick Suzie whatever we played Nintendo and shit then I went to work from 5:30 to 7:30, which was for some reason more grueling than usual ok b/c I had to teach this bunch of kids the breaststroke. Then like 12 of us went out w/Sherelle for her birthday. I wanted to go out w/Jonny instead b/c he was DJing this party but I decided Sher was a little more important. And it was a lot of fun and anyway I went home early.

Ok so today then was the SATs. It was soossososso awful. Billy drove me and this other kid over to the school Grimes and we actually got *LOST* for some

153

reason cause the directions were all fucked up and we were only half payin attention. Ok so then the actual test room and stuff it was not a good environment at all. The vocab section was really harder than I thought it would be. I may have done decent on the math but who knows considering what I got on that other test. I just really have no real idea how I did. It's like so unknown by me. And that kinda kills me ohhh well I hope I did good.

Ok so afterward we went over to this girl Deena's house she's in our grade and we were not even there for more than an hour when suddenly Deena goes oh my God there's like an accident outside like a car accident and someone just hit a sign or something and like 10 minutes later Micky Lazlo is screaming for me to come outside and I come outside and it's Marybeth standing there in tears. Emma got in an accident I guess she turned around to look at something and she just slammed totally into this bright red stop sign like hello? She didn't even hit the brake and stop.

Jake

March 21

I was at Deena's place last nite, she's this chick from our grade and we saw a car drive by and then *BLAM* we heard a smack and saw all these people running toward us. Me and Lazlo were the ones who

154

saw it first and then we realized who it was and we ran to the car, which was crushed right into this sign on the corner and totally trashed and totaled. Outside were Emma and her boyfriend and MB, and they were so upset. The whole front end was like indented and the worst part of all is that it was still running *AND* it was in drive! So I jumped in and turned the car off.

What happened was Emma was driving and was looking back at all these cars and so then she wasn't watching the road at all. That was why she hit the stupid sign. My reaction was, "Holy shit, how could that happen?!!!"

Emma

3/21, 1:00 p.m.

Last night I got into a car accident. I hit a stupid sign on the corner. Cliff and Marybeth were in the car with me. It was the scariest thing I have ever been through. It all happened so fast and I don't even really know what happened. We were driving by this girl Deena's house because we heard she was having a party and we wanted to see who was going to be there. Well, I was going around the bend and cars were parked on both sides and I was sort of in the middle of the road so I wouldn't hit them. Well, when I came back over to the right side of the road I misjudged the curb or something and veered off to the side and the next thing I know we crashed. The thing was that I never even saw the sign I swear it. I know Marybeth and Cliff saw it, and he said to me, "Look out," but I didn't know what he was talking about and then I hit it. My side had an air bag and it flew out. Cliff was so lucky because he was in the front and I hit on the passenger's side. But he and Marybeth both had their seat belts on. I totaled the car.

After I hit it, we all jumped out of the car so fast I didn't even turn it off. Jake and Kevin came outside and Jake was the one who turned off the car. I was in such shock and had no idea what to do. After like 5 minutes the cops came and I am not even sure who called them. Then Kevin called my dad from his cell phone. Thank God, Kevin and Jake were there and stayed with me. When the cops came they asked if everyone was ok and we said yes. I have a red thing on my neck I think from the air bag and Cliff has one big bruise on his side and Marybeth bruised her chest, but everyone was pretty much okay. No one went to the doctors or anything.

When the cops came they asked for my license, registration, and insurance and I didn't know where they were so I started panicking a little bit. But Jake was there then and he looked in the glove compartment and he found it in this stack of papers in there. Thank God. By then my dad had come and I totally ran to him and started crying actually I was more like screaming. Marybeth's mom came by too and she just held me. She kept saying that the car could be replaced but I couldn't be replaced. It helped me a little, but not really. I was still in so much shock about it all. The whole time I was standing there telling Kevin and Jake they could go away if they wanted but they didn't they stayed the whole time. Now I know they really do care about me. Then finally the cops asked me how this could have happened and I didn't really know what to say to them. Then he gave me a ticket because I had hit a sign and it belonged to the city so it was against the law or something like that and the ticket was for careless driving and 2 points on my license, which I have had for only about a month. My aunt is a lawyer and she says we can fight the ticket. I have to go to court on April 15 to do that. I told my mom I don't want another car because the truth is I am never ever driving again. I was just flipping out.

Whatever happens this entire experience will take me forever to pay back my mom. She says her friend has a used car she can get for very little money but still it will be more money than I can afford. Plus now I have the ticket to pay for and now my insurance payments are going to go up a lot. That was the part that my mom was upset about. She was mad actually, but now she is better. My neck is hurting a little bit but I am not saying anything. I do not want to have to go to the doctor. I don't even remember the air bag hitting me. Cliff and Marybeth said I put my hands up.

I just feel worse for Marybeth. This is her second accident in less than a month. And both times she was not the one driving. When we stepped out of the car she was crying so much I had no idea what to say to her at all.

Marybeth

March 21st

Well yesterday started out great anyway. I got tickets to Dave Matthews. Then last night I went out w/Em and Cliff. We were going to swing by that guy Teddy's house, the guy from work, but he wasn't home. So we decided to check out that girl Deena's party. She was having a house party and we had decided we wouldn't go but Emma still wanted to check out where she lived. Well we passed her house and that was it. Emma hit a freaking stop sign. Like that. We were going 30 mph at least and she just didn't see it there. Me and Cliff saw it as we hit it. It was seriously the scariest thing in my life so far. I just wish I hadn't been watching as we hit it. I wish I looked away or something. The air bag popped up and everything. Her car is totaled. My chest is bruised and I am in so much pain. My neck and legs and back are killing me. There's a huge bruise on my side too. I was in the backseat.

I drove today and was very defensive. I like drove

w/a completely different attitude. It was so weird. It really showed me yesterday how much can happen in just a single second.

Teresa

Mar 21

Dear Diary,

One minute I am dateless and the next minute—I have a prom date!!!! Emma's neighbor Doug asked me to go!!!! He is a *senior* and so I am going to sit at his table and go in his line instead of the junior line. I really don't mind *AT ALL*. I am just really really really happy that I found a prom date *FINALLY*. Plus I think he kinda likes me or at least that's what I have been told. I mean I only like him as a friend of course but he is really sweet and nice and I know we will have a good time. Emma is excited too!

This weekend (after the SATs . . . groan!) I went out with Sherelle a lot. She has a Mazda and she drives really really fast. It's fun though. We went to dinner with a group of people for her birthday. The only bad thing that we found out is that on Sat. nite Emma got into a car accident. Oh I feel sooooo bad for her because she has to pay so much money and now she has *NO* car!

Billy

I just got back from the repair shop—I had to bring the car in over the weekend. It needed a tune-up. Ok so now it's Monday and it's time for *RAW*.

This past week was so weird for me and for everyone. First off, on Friday nothing really happened. I didn't go to the movies like I wanted to. Just hung out at the mall and picked up a few ladies, with the whole crew of course. Sat. night was kinda cool because we had a party Anthony and Lexi held together at Lexi's place. Ladies, beer, the usual. I was looking around for those girls I like, Shauna or Olivia, but they were nowhere around, which sucked, and no one else looked good to me. Oh and I heard Emma crashed her car. Marybeth was in the car too. But they're ok. Well, my homework's done for the night so now *RAW* must be turned on. Later.

Kevin

3/23

Ok I couldn't write Sunday b/c I was so freakin busy and then I was so freakin tired. I did the same old thing for most of the weekend, went over to Jake's house and played video games and chilled. We looked through this mess of change he had been saving for like ten years in his room. We were trying to find a 1943 penny because they're worth like a million dollars.

Everyone's still freaked from the Sat. car crash but Mon. was still pretty boring and stupid Jonny & Jake didn't even go to school. That kinda sucked for me but ohh well. Later I had mad studying to do for chem, which I am doing bad in as we all know, so I tried to study but it was hard. I thought I knew most of the stuff but I could be wrong I hope I got at least a B.

Teresa

Mar 23

Dear Diary,

I am feeling soooo much better now that I know I have a date for the prom. Whew! I wasn't *really* worried but hey you never know. Anyway, Doug will be perfect for me. Okay I know this seems sooo weird, but just when I found out about Doug I saw this online somewhere—

Libras have a very strong need to form relationships and are never truly happy when alone. Often they see a relationship as giving them a sense of validity and identity. They have a great deal of loving to give to a partner and expect a lot in return. Venus's rulership of

**this sign imparts a sensuality and love of luxu-
rious surroundings. Libras adore setting the
scene for a romantic evening and will go to a
lot of trouble to make sure that the atmos-
phere is just right.**

Now is that a coincidence? Sometimes I get this
feeling like everything is lined up together. I can't believe that is a coincidence no way!!!! I am soooo glad
I waited. Thank you, Emma, for living next to this
guy!!!!

Marybeth

March 23rd

Well it's been a few days since the accident w/me
& Em. Today I went back to the doctors for my back
& neck from the accident. It sux. What am I gonna
do tho?

I was sorta offended too yesterday. Emma asked
me if we were gonna sue meaning like sue *her.* She
said she didn't know what would happen b/c we are
best friends and the whole thing was an accident.
Like did she really think I would do that? It was a
strange moment. I left school today at like 12 to go to
the doctor (chiropractor) and Baxter said that she
even said something to him at lunch about suing.
Anyway, the doctor took a lot of X rays & I have 2 go

back again tomorrow. He said I have really bad whiplash. It hurts a lot. I will eventually get better.

When I got back 2 school from the doc Emma wouldn't look at me or talk 2 me. I dunno why. I just don't understand. When I walked into this classroom everyone was all concerned asking me how my appt. went. Emma kind of ignored me though.

After school my friend and I went over to Matt's place. Then we went out for coffee and I went back to Matt's alone. It was funny because we started asking each other these questions and it seemed so serious like he asked me, "What is ur opinion of me?" and then I asked him too and he said we were just friends. So that's clear I guess. Anyway, we stayed talking for an hour or so more & then I came home. I am pretty drained since the whole accident happened.

I am not *glad* that I got into a bad car accident but the truth is that it has made me such a better driver. In all honesty I am like so much more alert! As of now I only have 28 more days until I get my full license.

Emma

3/24, 8:00 p.m.

Well I have gotten a little bit better since my accident. Yesterday everyone felt for me and kept asking me how I felt. It was nice and all but I wish people would just forget about it. Marybeth went to the doctor today, and I feel so bad, like really bad, and I don't even know what to say to her these days. I just feel that she is mad at me and I don't know why. I talked to Baxter about it but he told me I was crazy. Like I am afraid she's gonna blame me for the whole thing and sue me or something. I know she won't because our parents have been talking, but I feel way bad and I can't stop. I mean, I know she knows I didn't mean to do it but I feel like it is my fault.

My friend Pam has been very cool about the whole accident thing. She got into an accident too like a couple of weeks ago. She really knows how I feel. Like I don't mind if she asks me any questions or talks about it because I know she is really trying to help.

Yesterday before school the cops called me because they wanted my statements. I didn't know what to do because my aunt the lawyer said I shouldn't give one. I had to call her and she talked to the police officer. So then I had to go to the police station after school. I was so nervous and upset. I was also so pissed that the cop was treating me like shit. When I got to the station he said to me in this really obnoxious tone, "Ms. West, what's with the attitude?" I said I didn't have an attitude and he was like, yeah you sure do. I swear I was about to cry right there. He was really an asshole to me.

After I gave my statement he typed it up and by then my aunt was there at the station. She read it and told me not to sign it. The cop insisted that I was fooling around and stuff inside the car. That's what he wrote down. I wasn't. And when I wouldn't sign the statement he was like yelling at me and then I was going to cry again. He started talking to my aunt about this thing I can do to drop the points and my aunt and him were like getting along all of a sudden. She thinks he will do what she says. I just keep hoping.

When I got home there was a balloon sitting there waiting for me and attached was a note that said Cheer Up. They were from Cliff's mom. She sent me flowers too. The flowers came in a coffee mug that says Pick Me Up with this small bag of coffee too. I hate coffee but the thought was so nice. Cliff knew she was doing that too and he didn't even tell me. He's good at keeping secrets like that.

I just hope me and Marybeth start talking again soon. I feel so guilty and worried about her. Baxter says I should just stop already. Things will get better.

Baxter

March 24

I wish Emma and Marybeth would just deal with what happened the other day in the car. They are both acting so paranoid. For whatever reason they are talking about it to me. I feel like they should just relax. In a week or so everyone will be fine.

Here's the biggest news. I got a B+ in chemistry on this test. That is really good, especially since like no one did well on it. The teacher Mr. MacTaggart said the funniest thing today. He said the tests were mediocre, which for him is good, and that our ray diagrams sucked. He actually said "sucked." Just to hear that made him sound so funny. I laughed for hours.

Miss Shapiro aka *THE COW* or *THE BITCH*, depending on what day you ask me, has not apologized to me yet. She is clueless. Nothing matters as far as Community Club goes now, it is all shit. Nothing matters now. I heard she's not just mad at me. Apparently she's mad at *everyone*. She just makes everything harder. To be continued . . .

The Hardest Thing About Junior Year

Teresa:

Damn . . . everything about junior year is HARD!!!! First of all, accepting responsibility in the workplace and at school. I mean of course dealing with what college to go to and having to make a decision ourselves dealing with the rest of our lives! From sophomore year to junior year, one must do a great deal of growing up and dealing with the real world. For example, now that I work and have been in my job for 2 months, I have to take full responsibility of my money . . . it's gotta be the hardest thing to do!!! And what about work? This was my first year with AP classes and just feeling like an upperclassman was good but soooo scary. It is definitely a rude awakening. And then socially, people change most junior year. People grow up, learn from their mistakes, separate. Groups split or form and cliques take their status. It's very tumultuous. Junior year is ALL hard.

The Hardest Thing About Junior Year

Kevin:

Ohh mAn don't get me stARted. I think I miss it AlreAdy thAt feeling of eAse And freedom thAt I hAd in the beginning of the yeAR when I reAlly didn't hAve too mAny worries At All And reAlity didn't just set in And I don't think I Am reAlly reAdy for Adulthood And being A junior is like one step closer to All of thAt And life is just goin As I sAy All the time too f'ing fAst.

Katie:

It was such a shock in the beginning of the year to have such an increased workload but now that junior year is more than halfway through, I am less worried about the grade situation. So that has not, to my surprise, been the hardest thing about being a junior. I think maybe I am struggling the most with the fact that the social scene around me has changed so much. I feel stuck here sometimes, but I still know that I have to stick around for one more entire year. That makes it hard. You do all of this intensive preparation but then

The Hardest Thing About Junior Year

you just have to sit back and do senior
year and wait for colleges and there is a
lot of pressure associated with that for me.

Jake:

The hardest year yet. I feel like I
have to constantly prove myself.

Marybeth:

This junior yr. I started growing apart
from some friends, which wuz hard 4 me,
like Sherelle esp. I also am growing apart
from that whole scene w/The Mix but I
don't think that's such a bad thing. Mostly
the amount of work was the bad thing. But
even that was OK. I dunno—I like to see
the positive side if I can. Life is always
gonna b a little hard. . . .

Billy:

The extreme pressure on juniors for college
and all that is difficult. I mean I assume it is
because I feel it but I don't do anything about it.
I realize how important it is but I still can't do
my best and that's just the way it is. I think

The Hardest Thing About Junior Year

junior year is the hardest yet b/c you feel pressure and time catching up and you have to succeed and everyone is rushing and trying for the same thing. And what if you don't catch up and what if you don't succeed?

Emma:

Having to start thinking about colleges and the rest of my life is so hard for me. Last fall it was not such a big deal ya know wow I'm starting my junior year of high school and I wasn't even thinking twice about college but now as the spring is here I am realizing how much I have to do and start thinking about. What's hard is always worrying about all the work I can never get done.

Baxter:

This year's grades and classes decide your future. Plus now that we are almost done with junior year, I realize that I only have one more good year with my friends. That scares me a lot.

Jake

March 24

Well, I have been working all the time nonstop so whatever I can find to do after work or on the weekends then I will almost always do it. Most likely what I will do is go cruisin with Jonny.

Here is something that happened to me that was a big mistake. I hooked up with Suzie Wells, that girl from The Mix. It was a huge mistake actually. Then I hooked up with this other girl also in The Mix, Louise Gravas. She is very cute but she is a psycho. We were just talking at first and she was possessive of me then. Once we hooked up she got worse and worse. Then she had this manic-depression attack and she blamed it on me. She said she loved me and I never called her back. That's why she is depressed.

Seems to me like I am the one who should be depressed. This is all bullshit. I am thinking probably I will see Suzie again though if I can find time.

Teresa

Mar 25

Dear Diary,

It has been a lousy week and I have so much work and no time!! Anyway, last weekend's SATs weren't *that* bad but I have been thinking a lot over the last few days and I do not think that I reached my mark at all. I wanted a 1400. I definitely don't think I made that. I really don't know what I am doing this weekend other than thinking about how much better I could have and *should* have done on the SAT. What's wrong w/me?

I am going to a hockey game actually. That Irish kid Lawrence Gillooly who I was so into for a while back in the winter, who plays for the Redwood Reds, he is playing in the state finals on Sunday. Guess who is going to see him? *ME!!!!*

My dad is so cool. He got me tickets and so me and Dad are going to see Lawrence play. I hope the Reds win!!! Maybe I will get to see him up close again. I sure hope so!!!!!

Billy

3-25

This week coming up is going to suck. I gotta study my ass off this week. Study, study, study. Well, I always *say* I am gonna study but then I just sleep and decide to worry about it the next day. Oh well, I still am doing fine. Lacrosse is better. The arm is too. I talked to Lee tonite and he was saying all this nice stuff to me about doing well on the SATs and wanting me to go to U Michigan w/him. It was cool.

BTW since the play so many people have been

telling me I should sing more, which is so cool. It makes me feel really confident. I saw Olivia today and she said so too and she's in chorale so she would know. I guess you could say I am on the conceited side since I think I can do most anything these days.

Katie

March 25
@ 8:35 P.M.

What am I doing this week? *NOTHING!* Really nothing has happened lately. I feel like I was so busy and then all of a sudden it got called to a halt. I was playing a little bit of tennis and attending various meetings all week, though. I went to the movies with Brad. We haven't taken much time out together since the play; for some reason he is as busy as me. He is still really supportive, though. I am just waiting now to see what happened with the SATs and everything else.

Emma

3/25, 9:40 p.m.

Well, I just got done brushing my teeth and taking out my contacts. I am going to bed after I write. It's comfortable here. I haven't been feeling very comfortable lately that's for sure. I am so tired after all that has happened. Now I have a math *and* a chem quiz next week. I need a good grade on both of these, especially chemistry. I need to make my B– higher than it is. The end of the marking period is a week from today. And history is awful—my grades are so bad in that class. Everyone's grades are pretty bad, but they didn't send me a progress report so I have no idea what my final grade will be.

I just got off the phone with Cliff and he is being such a jerk! He has some German report due tomorrow and he hasn't done any of it. So now he is in such a bad mood and says it's my fault. Whatever. I told him to start that report on Monday and he didn't listen to me, so I am not to blame. I really hate it when he gets into these moods because then he doesn't really talk to me and then he yells and whatever. Tomorrow we are going to see this play at his school. Of course at the play will probably be all these other little girls who like him. I hate that. One of his friends who is in it wanted him to bring her a flower. I told him there was no way he was bringing a flower to her when he was going with me, he wouldn't do that.

The thing is, almost every girl in the play who is friends w/Cliff hates me and that's fine because I hate them too. The feeling is completely mutual. All I can say is they just better not say anything to me because I will go nuts. He's mine.

Today my mom told me I am going to get a new car. A new *CAR!* She said I have to have dual air bags in this one. She says I have to start driving again. I know once I get the car it will take some getting used to, like everything.

Katie

March 26
@ 9:10 P.M.

I got 1500!!!! I am so psyched, I feel like my heart won't stop beating! It was the most nervous minutes of my life when I was on the phone waiting to hear what my SAT scores were and it was so nerve-racking. After I put in a credit card number, the recording came on and it said, "Your scores for the March SAT test are: verbal—760. Percentile 98. Math—740. Percentile 96." I was so excited, I ran downstairs and tripped on the way down! I was yelling and jumping and my mom started going nuts when I told her and I almost knocked over a lamp. I am so thrilled and relieved and everything all at once. Strong SAT scores is like the missing link in a chain I started building three years ago. Now that I have achieved it, I can seriously begin considering schools. Brad got me some roses. He is very sweet. He didn't get his scores yet.

Emma

Just came back from Cliff's school play. I met all those girls I didn't want to meet. They are all really really ugly. This one in particular Jennie made a huge fool of herself. She was in the play and she dropped something onstage in the middle of the show and looked all stupid. I laughed hard but Cliff told me to stop. Then at the end after the play she came out from backstage and saw me with Cliff. She started complaining how she would not have dropped the prop if something else had gone better. I just kept staring right at her. I know she knew I was staring her down and I am glad she knew that. I am still convinced that Jennie has a thing for Cliff. I just think so.

But it didn't really matter because he was introducing me around to everyone as his girlfriend Emma. Now everyone knows who I am.

There was this other girl Sheila who said to me that she heard I had gotten into a bad car accident and I was like so what. I used to like her but now I am not too sure anymore. It's not like I see her all the time though so who really cares I guess.

Tomorrow will be 4 months for me and Cliff. I can't believe we are actually still together. Of course I am happy about it but things are going so well between the two of us that I can't really explain it. He has changed since the beginning of our relationship.

It's for the good. Like he tells me now how he feels about things and we talk so much more now about everything. We are really cute together or at least I think so. Well no, other people think so too. And my parents like him a lot. His mom likes me too. I know that because otherwise she never would have sent me that balloon and flowers.

Okay now it is late it's 12:04 and the phone just rang and it was guess who? Cliff! And he was calling to say that it was now officially our anniversary and wasn't that a cool thing. He remembered! He was like wow 4 months wow get excited now. That just made me really happy that he would say that. He does want to be with me. I have such a good feeling that we will be together for a long time.

Baxter

March 27

I feel like I have been depressed since the SATs were over. I think I am just tired actually, not depressed. The truth is I don't get depressed. I don't really see the point.

I have not really spent any time with Megan or Jessica lately. They are in school and all, but I just don't see them. I beeped them this past weekend but got no beeps back. Oh well, I guess they are just busy too. Everyone is.

Marybeth

March 27th

I am busy going to the chiropractor like *all* the time. I just went again tonite. I picked up Betsy and then Baxter afterward and the three of us hung out at my house tonite. We just chilled out. My back is still killing me. I have to be careful how I sit and lean and all that. It's hard to remember all the things I have 2 do! I was out of track and couldn't go to work either all week. The doctor just told me tonite that he wants me to wait another whole week to go back to them. That just sux 4 me. But there is like not much I can do about it except get well again.

Yesterday my friend from work came over here. Teddy came at about 4 and left around 7 at nite. He said he missed me at work. But right now what we have is just a friends thing. I mean, Ted is leading such a different life than me. He always gets in bad trouble! It would be pretty hard if I was in a relationship with him. And last nite when we were on the phone, he paid me these great compliments too. But it's just hard.

What Ted said wuz that he was having soooo much fun hanging out with me and he was completely sober doing it too. It's not like he's always drinking, but I think he does sometimes. Also, he said that he doesn't laugh at all and since he's been hanging more with me, he has been laughing. He says it's esp.

crazed b/c I am a girl *friend* and he doesn't usually feel that way except about girls he hooks ↑ with.

Ted says that where he is from you can't trust anyone and I wonder what that means. Really means. For some reason he says he can trust me completely w/everything. Ok it's late now.

Billy

3-27

It's around 1 on Saturday and I just got in like in the early a.m. I was just at this awesome party at this kid's house. It was like a drinking party and there was beer and ladies *EVERYWHERE*. There were people wild and stumbling everywhere. That is my definition of a good time. It was so great. Only thing is now I am really tired. And I have to get up for lacrosse practice in the morning.

Teresa

Mar 28

Dear Diary,

I got up so late today. I was exhausted! I straightened my hair yesterday because it was being so frizzy. Kevin told me he loves the way it looks and that made me feel so happy. But I don't think he meant it in any romantic way or anything. Only a few more days of school until spring break *YEAH*!!!

I cannot believe that I am still at my job @ KidCare. I feel like I just started there! I love what I do there soooooo much but I think I am undecided about whether it's what I want to do in college and all. Some days I do, some days I don't. That's not good—I need consistency!!

K evin

3/29

Only 3 more days until break ohh man I cannot wait I cannot wait. I am sooo bored and I like have been soooo bored like all term. I was just pissing around tonite. Life guarding wasn't happening this week so I didn't even have that to go to. Um no, life guarding is usually cool tho like my boss there is the bomb, she is so dope & I must admit I have hit on her and I mess w/her all the time. I would be psyched if she would hit back on me and we could hook up but who knows, right? I have been hanging with Jake a little less and Jonny some more but nothing major.

Jake

March 29

Well I am not having too much luck with the ladies as I have said in the past. And now I ain't drinking too much either. Once in a while I drink on the weekends but mostly I have been working at the mortgage co.

My dad has been real quiet lately, he says his medicine makes him tired. I keep trying to crack some jokes and shit. I have this need to make him feel ok. I feel really bad for what is happening. It just won't stop being hard. I had this heart-to-heart the other day with my history teacher, Mr. Bernstein. That means a lot to me.

I am glad spring break is soon.

Emma

3/31, 11:49 p.m.

So now we're on spring break and I like don't really know how to feel or what to think because everything has really changed since the accident. I feel this need to be around Cliff a lot because he is like the only person who is not judging me these days. I just hate how everyone else is like staring at me all the time and judging me whatever I do. I hate it so much.

I feel like the car accident has changed this year at school completely because everything started out one way and now they are becoming this other way. At lunch the other day too I overheard Katie talking and I was so pissed. She was saying something about my being irresponsible in the car or something. Well I didn't hear exactly but it sounded really bad. I was pissed!!!! I grabbed her in the hall and was like yelling for 5 minutes straight. She said it was a misunderstanding and then she just turned and walked away. Whatever.

I think that I hate junior year a little bit more than usual right now. I hate the fact that I got into that accident. I hate the fact that Sherelle is like totally off doing her own thing. I mean, she writes me notes in class now and then but mostly she never calls or beeps me. That makes me bummed out. I hate the fact that there is just so much pressure around me. I don't know how we can all handle all this pressure.

Real feelings. Real issues. Real life.

real teens

Diary of a Junior Year

VOLUME 6
COMING IN MAY 2000

Teen.

Real feelings. Real issues. Real life.

real teens

Teen.

$4.99 each!

real teens

Prom Sweepstakes

Win a prom dress or tuxedo, jewelry, a limousine, corsage or boutonniere, and pre-prom party for your friends!

What to Do: Just fill out the entry below and send it in for a chance to win!

YES. Enter me in the Real Teens Prom Sweepstakes.

Name_____ Date of Birth_____

Address_____

City_____ State_____ Zip_____

Phone (____)_____

SCHOLASTIC